TEAM PLAYERS

A **HOME TEAM** NOVEL

TEAM PLAYERS

MIKE LUPICA

SIMON & SCHUSTER BOOKS FOR YOUNG READERS
NEW YORK LONDON TORONTO SYDNEY NEW DELHI

SIMON & SCHUSTER BOOKS FOR YOUNG READERS
An imprint of Simon & Schuster Children's Publishing Division
1230 Avenue of the Americas, New York, New York 10020

SIMON & SCHUSTER BOOKS FOR YOUNG READERS
is a trademark of Simon & Schuster, Inc.
For information about special discounts for bulk purchases, please contact Simon
& Schuster Special Sales at 1-866-506-1949 or business@simonandschuster.com.
The Simon & Schuster Speakers Bureau can bring authors to your live event. For
more information or to book an event, contact the Simon & Schuster Speakers
Bureau at 1-866-248-3049 or visit our website at www.simonspeakers.com.
Book design by Lucy Ruth Cummins
The text for this book was set in Adobe Garamond Pro.
Manufactured in the United States of America
0318 FFG
First Edition
2 4 6 8 10 9 7 5 3 1
Library of Congress Cataloging-in-Publication Data Names:
Lupica, Mike, author.
Title: Team players / Mike Lupica.
Description: First edition. | New York : Simon & Schuster Books for
Young Readers, 2018. | Series: Home team | Summary: "A girl with Asperger's joins
Cassie's softball team but not everyone on the team welcomes her, creating a rift
between Cassie and her teammates"—Provided by publisher.
Identifiers: LCCN 2017022014 (print) | ISBN 9781481410090 (eBook) | ISBN
9781481410076 (hardback)
Subjects: | CYAC: Softball—Fiction. | Interpersonal relations—Fiction. | Asperger's
syndrome—Fiction. | Autism—Fiction. | BISAC: JUVENILE FICTION / Sports
& Recreation / General. | JUVENILE FICTION / Social Issues / Friendship. |
JUVENILE FICTION / Social Issues / General (see also headings under Family).
Classification: LCC PZ7.L97914 (ebook) | LCC PZ7.L97914 Te 2018 (print) |
DDC [Fic]—dc23
LC record available at https://lccn.loc.gov/2017022014

This book is for Teri Thompson

TEAM PLAYERS

BEFORE THE SEASON . . .

ONE

It wasn't as if Cassie Bennett were looking to make any new friends that summer.

She definitely wasn't looking to lose any.

She ended up doing both.

DURING THE SEASON . . .

TWO

As weird as it sounded, sometimes Cassie felt as if managing the friends she had, in school and in sports, were like having a full-time job.

Cassie had her classmates at Walton Middle, where the school year had ended the previous Friday. She was about to have her softball teammates, as the All-Star League in their part of the state was about to begin.

Some of her classmates were teammates, but not all.

On top of all that, she had her best friends in the world, Jack Callahan and Teddy Madden, Gus Morales, and his twin sister, Angela. Though, Angela wasn't around right now. She'd signed up for Walton's Teen Abroad program, and was spending most of the next two months staying with a family in Barcelona to study art.

For now her friendship with Angela involved Skype and FaceTiming. Cassie spent a lot of their conversations offering to pay Angela to stop speaking Spanish as often as she did.

"I get it," Cassie had said to her last night on Skype. "You're not just having an adventure without me. You're having it in your second language."

"Technically," Angela said, "and as much as I know you hate being corrected, Spanish is my first language."

Her parents had been born in the Dominican Republic, and both Gus and Angela had spoken Spanish before they'd spoken English.

"All I know," Cassie said, "is that now you're annoying me in both languages."

"*De nada*," Angela said, smiling at Cassie through cyberspace, and from across the world, telling Cassie, "You're welcome."

"*Cállate*," Cassie said.

Shut up.

She'd been saving that one.

Angela laughed, said they'd talk in a couple of days, and cut the connection.

Cassie knew she was lucky to have the friends she did. She was even smart enough to know by eighth grade that there was nothing more important—at least outside family—than being a good friend and being able to count on your friends, no matter what. She knew more about that than ever before because of the way her friendship had been tested during the previous basketball season, after Cassie had tried out for, and made, the boys' town team, the Warriors. Gus hadn't wanted her on the team at first, and for most of the season. He'd gotten mad at her, she'd gotten mad at him, and they'd both dug in. It had sometimes seemed as if they weren't going to be able to work through all that, and that the friendship might really be gone. There were times when Cassie was sure she'd lost Gus for good. But they had made it through. They had worked it out, both on and off the court, as stubborn as she was and as stubborn as he was.

In the end, it was what friends did. They were able to figure things out even when one of them thought the other was being as dumb as a sock drawer.

But it seriously did feel like too much of a full-time job sometimes, having a lot of friends. Or just too much responsibility.

TEAM PLAYERS

If somebody texted you and you didn't text them back right away, it could quickly turn into a thing. If one of her girlfriends posted a picture on Instagram and Cassie didn't immediately slap a *like* on it, pretty soon that was a thing. Or if she wasn't involved enough when there was a group chat.

All sorts of things could be *things*.

It made Cassie giggle sometimes when she thought of it that way, as if she were starring in a Dr. Seuss story.

But Cassie was smart enough to know that a lot of the pressure she was feeling was because of who she was. She was the best girl athlete her age in Walton, maybe any age, and because she'd just shown everybody in town that she could hold her own with the boys, it was as if people were watching her more closely than ever. It put even more pressure on her not to act as if she were big-timing her friends, almost as if there were one set of rules for her and another for everybody else.

She was trying to explain that to Jack and Teddy and Gus at lunch on Monday, at their favorite pizza place in Walton, Fierro's.

"No question," Teddy said. "It's hard being you."

"*Cállate,*" she said.

When you get a good thing, stay with it.

"Excuse me?" he said.

"It means 'shut it' in Spanish."

Teddy grinned across the table at Jack and Gus. "Help me out here," he said. "Don't we talk about how hard it is being her?"

"I think she just manages by being so cool," Gus said.

He was grinning too, but at Cassie.

She leaned forward across the table and gave him what they all called the Look. "Your sister isn't around to protect you," she said. "Keep that in mind."

"You know," Gus said, "that is an excellent point right there. Why don't I *cállate* and finish my delicious slice."

"I'm actually trying to make a serious point here," Teddy said. "People wanted to hang with you before the basketball season. But now that you became the Mo'ne Davis of the boys' team, you're like a rock star."

Mo'ne Davis, they all knew, was the girl from Philadelphia who'd been the star pitcher on a boys' baseball team that had made it all the way to the Little League World Series a few years ago.

"Wait," Jack Callahan said. "You mean Cass wasn't a rock star already?"

"I wasn't trying to prove a point in basketball," she said. "I just wanted to play point guard."

"Yeah," Teddy said, "go with that." Then Jack and Gus were trying to make laughs sound like coughs, and Teddy was doing the same thing, and somehow Cassie, being Cassie, was able to give them all a withering glance at the same time.

"Maybe," she said, "instead of managing all the friends I have in my life, I just could lose three right now."

"You know that is a big old no-can-do," Jack said. "We're a team."

They'd always called themselves the "Home Team." And they had been through a lot together, over the past year or so. The rest of them had helped Jack through the death of his older brother, Brad, who'd died in a dirt-bike accident. They'd all helped Teddy get into shape and overcome obesity, and also deal with his divorced dad coming back into his life unannounced. Then all four of them had survived what had happened between Gus and Cassie during the basketball season. It really was a lot. But they were a team.

More important, they were friends.

"You know what they say in sports every time a coach or manager gets fired," Teddy said. "You can't fire the whole team."

She leaned forward again and said, "Watch me, funny man."

"You know," Teddy said, and not for the first time, "that look doesn't scare me nearly as much as it used to."

"But it still scares you," Jack said.

"Oh, totally," Teddy said.

"You know what your problem is?" Cassie said. "You just have no idea what it's like to be a girl, do you?"

Jack looked at Gus. "Is there really a good answer to that question?"

Gus, mouth full of pizza, slowly shook his head from side to side.

"Wait a second," Jack said. "Aren't you the one always telling us that girls are smarter and cooler than boys?"

"I am," Cassie said. "Just not all girls. It's just that sometimes they can act dumber than, well, *boys*."

"Hey," Teddy said. "We're doing the best we can."

"I know," she said. "It's kind of sad."

"Here's what I don't get," Jack said. "When you do have girls acting even dumber than guys, when they're worrying about stuff you don't worry about, why do you worry about that?"

Teddy, frowning, turned to Gus and said, "You know, I think I actually followed that."

"When you're a guy and a girl doesn't talk to you, it might upset you, but you deal with it," Cassie said. "But sometimes with other girls, you just can't avoid the drama, even if it's something as small as not talking or even not nodding to one of them when I pass them in the hall at school. Or if one of them or all of them has decided that I've spent too many days in a row sitting with you guys at lunch and not them. I mean, like, get over it!"

"I get it," Jack said.

"Like I said," she said, "it's not all girls. Just a small group of them."

"But they're still your friends," Jack said.

"And if they are, they shouldn't have to worry about me being there for them if they need me."

Gus said, "Heck, I know that better than anybody now, even if I had to find out the hard way."

She leaned over and pinched the upper part of his arm.

"I hate when you do that," Gus said.

"If you didn't hate it," she said, "what fun would it *be* to do that?"

She took a bite of her own slice of pizza, then washed it down with some water. Then she frowned and shook her head.

"You know that expression our parents are always using about not sweating the small stuff?" she said. "I think they should change it to not sweating the stupid stuff. Girls *or* boys."

She had no way of knowing at lunch that day how much truly stupid stuff she was about to encounter.

She had *absolutely* no idea that she was about to learn more about friendship—and who her friends really were—than she ever had before.

THREE

Her name was Sarah, and right away Cassie knew there was something different about her. But that was before anybody saw her run down a ball in the outfield, or throw, or swing a bat.

"She's special," Cassie's dad told her before softball tryouts began that night.

"Are you talking about special needs, Dad?" Cassie said. "We've had a bunch of special-needs kids at school."

"Just special," her dad said. "Think of her that way, same as her parents do. You'll see."

"How do you know?"

"I met her parents and Sarah at the field yesterday," her dad said, "and worked her out a little bit, and tried to get to know her."

"You didn't tell me," Cassie said.

Her dad grinned. "Must've slipped my mind."

"Dad," Cassie said, "nothing ever slips your mind."

"Trust me," he said. "You're gonna be happy she's on our team. You and the other girls are just going to have to give her a little room at first."

Cassie was sure that nothing, not even a new girl, was going to change how happy she was to be back on a baseball field again. She loved soccer and loved basketball, girls' or boys' basketball. She had always loved competing. And loved to win, whatever the sport. There was just something about softball, whether she was pitching or hitting or playing shortstop, that she loved most of all.

But it was hard not to notice the new girl, who'd been standing alone in the outfield, glove on her left hand, from the moment she'd taken the field, waiting for batting practice to begin.

She hadn't spoken to any of the other girls yet. As far as

Cassie could tell, she hadn't even looked at any of them. Cassie wasn't watching her every minute, but when she did look out there, Sarah was simply staring down at the outfield grass.

Until the first ball was hit in her direction.

Lizzie Hartong, who'd been the third baseman on last year's team, the Orioles, and was expected to play the same position this year, was the first batter of the night. Cassie's dad was pitching to her.

"Heads up, everybody. Good hitter," Chris Bennett yelled.

Cassie saw Sarah pick her head up then, still in the same spot in right-center field, saw her react to the ball coming off Lizzie's bat like a rocket, Lizzie's first big swing of the summer, the ball looking as if it were on its way toward the wall in left-center, or maybe over it.

Cassie, waiting to hit after Lizzie, watched Sarah take off to her right, covering an amazing amount of ground on her long legs even though she didn't seem to be running her hardest, her eyes tracking the ball, focused only on that. But even with the great jump she'd gotten, Cassie thought there was no way she could outrun Lizzie's ball.

But she did.

She didn't put up her glove hand, reaching across her body, until the last possible second, maybe ten feet away from the Dunkin' Donuts sign on the wall in left-center. She stretched across her body, and reached for the sky with her glove, made the backhand catch, stopped herself a few feet short of the wall, pivoted, and made a perfect throw to Allie Gordon at second base.

As soon as Sarah had made the throw, she ran back to the exact same spot in right-center, head back down.

Cassie felt her dad looking at her from the pitcher's mound. He was smiling as he mouthed the words, *Told you.*

Cassie smiled back at him, and nodded.

They'd talk later, at home, about autism and about Asperger's syndrome, the developmental disorder on the autism spectrum— the disorder with which Sarah Milligan had been born.

For now, though, on the field at Highland Park, Cassie understood what her father had meant when he'd called Sarah special.

She could hit, too.

And she could pitch.

She couldn't pitch as fast, or as well, as Cassie Bennett could. But when Cassie's dad went behind the plate and got into a catcher's crouch and told Sarah to cut loose, Cassie saw the way the ball exploded out of her right hand, and how natural her windmill motion looked. Cassie heard the sound the softball made in her dad's old catcher's mitt.

"She's weird, but she's really good," Kathleen Timmins, their left fielder last season, said to Cassie.

Cassie grinned. "Wait," she said, "that sounds exactly like you."

"Funny."

"I'm sorry," Cassie said. "I can't help myself."

"Is she really going to play on our team?" Nell Green said.

"You've been watching tryouts," Cassie said to her. "What do you think?"

Kathleen said, "She doesn't talk."

Cassie said, "With the way our team talked last year, that's probably a good thing. A blessing, even."

They were halfway through tryouts. Everybody had batted by now and gone through some basic baserunning drills. Cassie's dad and Allie's dad were about to separate the outfielders from the infielders and have them all take the field. Cassie was a shortstop when she wasn't pitching, but before the fielding drills began, she ran out to where Sarah was standing in right-center, alone. Cassie's dad hadn't told the other girls what he'd told Cassie, about giving Sarah room.

But the other outfielders were doing just that, almost as if they were afraid to approach her, like there was some sort of force field around her, less than an hour into the new season.

Cassie ran straight to where Sarah was standing, the exact

same spot to which she returned every time after she had caught a fly ball during batting practice.

"I'm Cassie," she said, and put out her hand.

Cassie couldn't tell whether Sarah looked startled or just plain frightened at first. But she finally put out her own right hand, just the way you would if you were afraid you might be touching a hot plate.

She didn't look at Cassie as she did, staring past her, like she was fixed on some spot in the infield.

"Sarah," she said.

"That was some catch you made at the start of tryouts," Cassie said.

She was looking right at Sarah. Sarah was still looking in the direction of home plate, or maybe downtown Walton.

Sarah didn't respond, just kept shifting her weight from one foot to the other.

Cassie wasn't giving up.

"How long have you been playing?" she said.

"I never played," she said.

Then she was running again, not after a ball in the air this time, just running toward first base, then past first base. Cassie was afraid she might be running right off the field, like she might be thinking about running all the way home. But when she got to the bench, she suddenly sat at the end of it, head still down, alone.

Cassie wasn't sure if she understood. No, she was *sure* she didn't understand Sarah, at least not yet, and maybe not ever. But it wasn't as if Sarah didn't want to be around other people. It just seemed that she didn't know how to act when she was.

She didn't want to be alone. But didn't know how not to be.

FOUR

When they got home, Cassie's dad told her as much as he said he knew about Asperger's, at least for now.

"You remember back in fifth grade," Chris Bennett said to his daughter, "that boy Peter Rizzo, who had autism?"

"Peter didn't speak at all," Cassie said. "But the thing I remember best is how smart he was, especially in math. I used to wish I was nearly as good at math as he was."

They were in the living room. Cassie's mom was out to dinner with Jack's mom, and Teddy's.

"I was trying to explain to you before," her dad said, "about the autism spectrum. The higher you are on it, the better able you are to function in school, or really in the world."

Cassie had only had a couple of classes with Peter Rizzo that year, before he and his family had moved to Texas. Something else she remembered about him—when he'd get frustrated with something in class, even in math, he would just suddenly get up and leave the classroom. And she remembered how frustrated that had made her feel. She'd felt as if there ought to be something she could do to help him, or reach him, make him feel more accepted. Or safe, even. She would try to sit with him sometimes at lunch, because she felt bad when she saw him eating alone, but even that was awkward, because she felt as if she were talking to herself.

One day she'd come home from school, nearly in tears, and said to her mom, *"Why can't I fix this?"*

And her mom had said, "Because this isn't something you or anybody else can fix. It's who Peter is. And he doesn't think he needs fixing. His normal just happens to be different from yours."

Cassie's dad told her now that Sarah had only played

basketball before this, starting with a Special Olympics Unified Sports team, on which some of the players were mentally challenged and some weren't. According to Cassie's dad, it was Sarah's being on that team originally, back in the sixth grade, and turning out to be as gifted an athlete as she was, that had helped her coaches realize that she had far more social skills than they'd originally thought.

"By last year," Chris Bennett said, "she was the star of a team that went all the way to the Special Olympics World Games. And she'd gotten so good at basketball, she was the one partnering with more challenged kids, the way she'd been partnered herself when she'd started playing ball."

"But that means she had to talk to them," Cassie said. "You saw what happened tonight when I tried to talk to her. It was like I'd chased her away."

"Her parents say it takes time for her to feel safe when she gets thrown into a new situation," her dad said. "Now she's living in a new town, meeting new people, playing a new sport. It's going to take time, and a lot of effort, mostly on our part."

It turned out that there were no softball teams in Special Olympics for girls her age. But her dad, just from playing in the yard with her, and then taking her to a local field, had come to see how much she loved softball, and how good she might be at it.

"Really good," Cassie said. "Mad good."

Their seventh-grade team, the Orioles, also coached by Cassie's dad, had gone undefeated and had won every tournament in the state that a girls' softball team could win. And they all knew that this summer the stakes were even higher for them. If they could win their All-Star League, they qualified for a New England tournament that would be shown on NESN, the Red Sox television network, with the championship game at Fenway Park on a weekend in August when the Red Sox were on the road. It wasn't the Little League World Series. But it would do.

The teams that were good enough would get their chance to play at Fenway, and get their chance to play on television. Yeah, that kind of spotlight would do, all of them getting their chance to shine. It was the biggest reason why Walton Baseball had asked Cassie's dad to come back and coach one more season, even though he'd sworn he was retiring last year.

Cassie's dad told her he'd been reading up on Asperger's since Sarah's mom and dad had called and asked to meet with him. Not only did her parents want Sarah to play softball, but they planned on enrolling her at Walton Middle in the fall.

"I'm not trying to give you the same crash course on Asperger's I'm giving myself," Cassie's dad said. "But the thing that can be most difficult for these kids is what we think of as normal social interaction."

"Like just complimenting her on a good play in the outfield," she said.

"Like that."

He said it wasn't going to be the last time that Sarah might panic and run away, and she might not even stop at the bench next time. Or she might lose her temper, because her parents said she could fly off the handle, sometimes for reasons that only she understood. Or she could get fixed on routines, like standing in the same spot in the outfield.

"She didn't make much eye contact tonight, Dad."

"And she might not. And there might be things that make no sense to you. Her parents said that even though loud noises bother her, she can get loud sometimes."

"Sounds like a process," Cassie said.

"And a challenge for you," her dad said. "But who's more up for challenges than you are?"

"You got me there," she said, and bumped him some fist.

"Listen," he said, "this whole thing is gonna be a work in progress, for me included. For all of us. But I'm gonna need your help to make it work."

"Just tell me how."

"With some of the other girls," he said. "The ones who, let's face it, aren't always as aware about stuff as you are. I mean, I know a lot of people think you're stuck on yourself—"

"Hey," Cassie said. "I thought we were bonding here."

He laughed. "But I know better, because I know my daughter. And her heart. It's why I know you can take the lead on this."

"Sounds like you're setting the bar kind of high for me, Dad."

He smiled. It was the kind of smile that had always felt to Cassie like his arms around her. "Almost as high as you set it for yourself."

They sat in silence for a moment, the only sound in the room the ticking of their antique grandfather clock, actually given to them by Cassie's grandfather.

"I promise this will be worth it," her dad said.

Then he added, "Win or lose."

Cassie felt herself smiling. "I know," she said. "So she's going to make the team, then?"

Chris Bennett laughed again, even louder than before.

"She made it when she caught that ball," he said.

When they were finished, Cassie went upstairs and got out her laptop and read up on Asperger's syndrome herself, starting with the Autism Speaks website. She was trying to understand about the autism spectrum, telling herself to think of it as a scale and not a spectrum. But what was pretty clear to her was some of the behavior you could expect from somebody with

Asperger's, some of the awkward mannerisms, some of the things her dad had mentioned and some he hadn't.

There was one thing that jumped out at her and actually made her smile, though she knew none of this was funny:

"One-sided conversations."

When she called Jack and told him about that one, he said, "One-sided conversations? That sounds like half the kids we know. Heck, probably more than half."

Cassie said, "There was also this thing about kids with Asperger's sometimes being obsessed with unusual topics."

Jack said, "That sounds like your whole team."

"But honestly?" she said. "This is no joke. Kathleen and Nell? You know what they're really obsessed with? Being good enough this season to get on television. No lie, Jack. They think that if they can do that, they'll be halfway to being Kardashians."

Jack wanted to know more about Sarah, what she'd been like at practice. Cassie told him about her standing in one place, and no eye contact, and running away when Cassie had tried to talk to her. But then Cassie told him about the catch she'd made, and how she'd turned and thrown the ball back in, even though she'd never played in a real softball game in her life, like she just instinctively knew that was the right thing to do. And then Cassie told him about what Sarah had been like when it was her turn to bat, how nervous she'd looked at the start, as if she'd known that everybody was watching her, how she'd swung and missed badly on the first few pitches Cassie's dad had thrown to her.

After that, though, she'd proceeded to hit a line drive over third base, another one over first, hit a ball off the wall in right-center, and nearly took Chris Bennett's head off with a shot right back up the middle.

"So she can really play?" Jack said.

"*Yeah,*" Cassie said.

"Did she pitch?"

"*Oh yeah,*" Cassie said.

"As fast as you?"

Cassie said, "I'm not going to dignify that with a response."

"I don't know what I was thinking," Jack said.

Then he said, "If she's as good as you say she is, then it should be no problem with the other girls, because she'll just make your team better, right?"

"I just want everybody on the team to be nice to her."

"Because she's a good player, or because she's a good person?" Jack said.

Cassie paused, because it was such a good question.

"Hopefully both," she said.

"Listen, Cass," Jack said, "it's going to be like everything else. They'll take their lead from you, like they do on the field.

Because they know they have no chance to make it near Fenway without you."

"You're probably right."

"I'm calling Teddy and Gus and telling them you told me I was right about something."

"I said 'probably.'"

"You're probably overthinking this," he said.

"Okay, what do you think about this—or overthink—is it going to work out?"

"Honestly? I have no clue. And no matter what you do, and how easy you try to make things for her, you can only play your own game. You can't play hers."

"Who says?" Cassie Bennett said.

FIVE

Sarah made the team.

All of the girls from last year's team made it too, at least the ones who still lived in Walton. Two had moved away. But the best players were still around, Brooke behind the plate, Lizzie at third base, Allie at second, same as when they'd gone undefeated. Nell was still in right field, Kathleen in left. Greta Zahn had played center last season and had thought she was going to play center this season. But Cassie was sure that was going to change now that Sarah Milligan was on the team, which was going to be called the Red Sox. Sarah was a better fielder than Greta, a better batter. A better everything.

When they had their first practice after the team was set, the Tuesday after tryouts and four days before the season would officially begin, Sarah still didn't seem to be more comfortable with her new teammates. It didn't stop her, though, from making another spectacular catch during batting practice, this one on a ball that Brooke had hit, Sarah coming in on a sinking line drive and making a sliding, backhand play.

"She's like a one-girl highlight film," Cassie said to Greta.

They were both waiting to hit.

"Anybody can make plays in practice," Greta said.

Greta was tall and blond. She was fast and had surprising power for someone as skinny as she was. But just from one tryout and the start of practice tonight, anybody could see she wasn't the ballplayer that Sarah Milligan was, whether this was Sarah's first time on a team or not.

"I have this feeling," Cassie said to Greta, "that she's going to be one of those players who does what my dad says we're supposed to do: practices like she plays."

"It sounds like you're cool with her creepiness," Greta said.

Cassie turned to her, leaning on her bat.

"Gonna give you a heads-up, Zahn," Cassie said, smiling but

not meaning it. "I wouldn't let our coach—my dad—hear you calling Sarah creepy."

"Would you feel better if I called her weird?"

"Not so much."

"So you're telling me you don't think it's going to be weird having her around?"

Cassie had always managed to get along with Greta, who was probably the smartest kid, boy or girl, in their grade at Walton Middle. But having known her since kindergarten, Cassie also knew that Greta was never going to get an A in being kind.

Cassie gave Greta her biggest smile now and said, "We've only known her for two days. What I think would be weird is not giving her a chance to fit in."

And she walked up to the plate to get her swings.

Even though they'd only spent two days around Sarah, they all could see by now how much she liked routine. *Really* liked routine. It wasn't just that she was always in the same spot in the outfield. When Sarah did speak to Cassie's dad, she wanted to know what the batting order was for batting practice, exactly when she'd be hitting, who was going before her and who was going afterward. She always placed her bat bag in the exact same spot where she'd left it during tryouts, underneath their bench, at the end closest to home plate.

When they'd watched her place it there tonight, Kathleen had said, "She's like a softball neat freak."

"Wade Boggs, who used to play for the real Red Sox, ate chicken at the same time before every game," Cassie said. "And he's in the Baseball Hall of Fame."

This was before they'd all taken the field. Sarah had been sitting at the end of the bench, by herself, where the bat bag was.

"Look at her," Kathleen said, at least keeping her voice low. "It's like she's on the team and not on the team at the same time."

"C'mon, Kath," Cassie said. "You've seen her play. You don't think she's gonna help us?"

"I didn't know we needed help."

"You can always get better," Cassie said. "Do you know who Kevin Durant is?"

"No."

"Never mind," Cassie said.

"I just don't want anything to get in our way this season," Kathleen said. "Or anybody."

"Maybe we should all just concentrate on staying out of our own way," Cassie said. "And remembering that being on this team is supposed to be fun."

Kathleen nodded at Sarah. "Does she look as if she's having any?" she said.

MIKE LUPICA

They did some baserunning drills after everybody had gotten their swings during batting practice. Cassie's dad would put runners on first and second, or first and third. Sometimes he would load the bases. Then he'd tell them how many outs there were, maybe even make up a game score and an inning, before he'd hit a ball to one of the outfielders. Sometimes it would be a base hit, sometimes a fly ball. Sometimes one of them would try to score from third on a fly ball, or just take an extra base. It went like that. He kept rotating the outfielders. But by now everybody had figured out that if the ball was hit to Sarah, it was a losing play to try to run on her arm.

One time Cassie was on second base and Chris Bennett hit a hard single to Sarah in center. Her dad had announced that there were two outs, so Cassie was running as soon as he hit the ball. As she came around third, she was able to pick up Sarah's throw to the plate with her eyes, saw it tracking toward Brooke behind the plate. As fast as Cassie was, she wasn't fast enough to outrun a throw that ended up in Brooke's mitt on the fly.

Cassie was out by ten feet.

She's a freak, Cassie thought.

In a good way. A sports way.

Kathleen had scored from third ahead of Cassie on the play, and was standing next to the plate when Brooke easily tagged out Cassie.

TEAM PLAYERS

Cassie shook her head and said to Kathleen, "She might not *look* as if she's having any fun out there. But I'll bet it's fun to throw a ball like that."

Kathleen just stared at her. "What is she, your new best friend?"

"Just a new teammate," Cassie said, before she went to get her glove and run out to shortstop.

"Not the same thing," Kathleen called after her.

Cassie ran right past her and said, "To me, it is."

Because the season was starting on Saturday, Cassie's dad had scheduled practices for the next two nights. Jack and Teddy and Gus were coming to Highland Park on Thursday night. When practice was over, around seven o'clock, they all planned to walk into town and have pizza at Fierro's.

Cassie had told them she could just meet them, but Jack had said, "We want to see NG."

New Girl. Sarah.

"What about me?" Cassie said.

"Of course we always want to watch you," Jack said.

"Just remember that means watch, and not make observations I can hear," she said.

They had finished playing two-on-two basketball at the hoop in Cassie's driveway and were now in the car with Cassie's mom on their way to the field. Baseball All-Stars for the guys didn't start for another week, and Jack and Teddy and Gus had worked out a little at Walton Middle in the morning, something they loved doing now that school was out. But they said that if they didn't have some real competition, they were going to go crazy. So it had been Jack and Cassie today against the other two, with Jack and Cassie crushing them.

Teddy said, "But if we make amusing observations you can't hear, that doesn't count against us, right?"

Cassie said, "I'll know you're making them."

"But you won't know exactly what we're saying," Gus said.

Mrs. Bennett said, "I wouldn't be so sure of that."

Jack said, "We know what you can do, Cass. We do want to see the new girl."

"Is she fitting in any better?" Gus asked.

"Not even a little bit," Cassie said.

"What does she do?" Teddy asked.

"Hits and runs and catches and throws," Cassie said. "Then one of her parents or both of her parents pick her up and she goes home."

There was a time, back when Cassie first started playing team sports, when practice felt like homework to her. Like a chore. But not anymore. There had been a night last season when her dad had pulled her aside after practice, when it had been clear to everybody, starting with her dad, that she had just been going through the motions. She'd been goofing around on the field, even batting left-handed when it was her last turn to hit, showing off for her teammates, nearly hitting a home run.

Before they'd even gotten into the car, Chris Bennett had walked her down the right-field line, away from the rest of the Orioles, and said, "What were you doing out there tonight?"

"Having fun."

"You're the best player on this team, and you know it," he said. "If you don't take this stuff seriously, none of your teammates will either."

"I'm always serious once the game starts," she said, knowing how defensive she sounded.

"I want you to be serious when I'm trying to teach the team how to play this game the right way," he said. "So I can't have you going the wrong way. Somebody told me once that when your best player does things the right way, it filters down through every other player on the team."

"You know I play the right way, Dad."

"Not tonight you didn't," he said.

She had taken what he'd said to heart. Ever since, she had run out every ball at practice, taken every drill seriously, even leading some of them when her dad asked her to. She had done her best to practice like she played. She knew it wasn't a real game,

MIKE LUPICA

knew that every swing she took and every ball she fielded and every pitch she threw didn't matter the way they did when the games counted. But she had discovered something: there were all kinds of ways to have fun in sports. And now the harder she worked, the more fun she had.

She had told that to her dad after the first official practice for the Red Sox.

He'd put a hand to his chest and staggered back a couple of steps. "You're telling me I was right?" he said.

"I'll tell you what I tell Jack and the guys," she'd said, smiling at him. "Don't let it go to your head."

There were thirteen players on the team, which meant they didn't have enough to scrimmage. So when Cassie and the guys got to the field, her dad announced that he was putting Jack and Teddy and Gus to work. He needed them to be players, because he wanted to have a three-inning scrimmage, with him pitching for both teams.

"And which position would you like to play on Cassie's team?" Mr. Bennett said to Jack.

Jack was grinning at Cassie when he said, "Shortstop?"

Her position.

"Very funny," Cassie said.

Brooke jumped in and said, "You catch for my team, Jack. I'll go play the outfield for theirs."

"I'd rather play against Cassie anyway," Jack said.

"Your loss," Cassie said.

Cassie's team was starting in the field. Sarah was on Cassie's team, playing center. Cassie had watched her when her dad had brought Jack and Teddy and Gus out onto the field. She didn't look frightened, exactly, at three boys she didn't know basically joining the Red Sox tonight. She didn't look angry. There was just a look of wariness on her face, as if somebody had moved her stuff.

Cassie had said hardly anything to Sarah over the past couple of practices, still giving her space. Or maybe not trying to invade her space. But now, watching as Sarah kept staring at the guys, she walked over and quietly said, "It's okay. They're friends of mine."

Sarah's response was to sprint out to her position.

The scrimmage, their first, was fun. Because it was a three-inning game, it meant that everybody would likely get one at bat. By the bottom of the third, last ups for Cassie's team, they were losing 4–3. Jack, who could have been a switch-hitter, same as Cassie, had hit one over Sarah's head in the top of the third, knocking home two runs and putting his team ahead.

"You figured me out," Cassie's dad said to him when Jack was standing on second base. "In one at bat."

"Up and in, low and away, then up and in," Jack said.

"You don't miss much," Chris Bennett said.

"He's cocky enough already, Dad," Cassie said from short.

"Look who's talking," Jack said.

Cassie's dad looked at his daughter, then at Jack, and said, "So it goes."

He got two quick outs in the bottom of the third. Greta popped out, and then Kathleen hit one hard, but directly at Teddy in right field.

When he threw the ball back in, he yelled to Cassie, "Am I about to get my first-ever win in girls' softball?"

Cassie was walking to the plate. She yelled back, "I'm sorry, is the game over yet?"

"About to be," Teddy said.

Cassie thought: *I never make the last out, not even in a scrimmage. And I'm not doing it tonight with my boys in the game.*

"That was a mistake," Jack said from behind the plate. "Him chirping you."

"Always," Cassie said, taking her stance, setting her hands, staring out at her dad.

She ripped the first pitch she saw from him over Lizzie's head at third base, down the left-field line, and into the corner, before Brooke finally ran it down and got the ball back into the infield.

Cassie thought she might have been able to make third. But

she wasn't *sure* she could make it. And you didn't make the last out of the game at third, even if it was a scrimmage.

Practice like you play.

But once she was at second base, and the ball was back in her dad's glove, she did find the time to stare out at Teddy in right, and put a hand to her ear, like she couldn't hear anything. Chirping him right back without saying a word. Teddy acted like he couldn't see, just turned to his other outfielders and made a motion with his fingers, reminding them there were still two outs.

Sarah came to the plate. She didn't say anything to Jack, or look at him as she dug in. Cassie watched as Sarah went through the same exact routine she did before every swing. She leaned forward and touched the far side of the plate three times with the end of her bat. She tugged the right shoulder of her T-shirt, then the left shoulder. Tugged on the bill of her cap. Then, and only then, did she look out at the pitcher.

Her first time up against Mr. Bennett, she'd hit a ball so hard back up the middle that it had gone through his legs before he'd had time to get his glove down. Now, in her stance, she was completely still, the way she always was. Cassie liked to wave her bat a little before the pitch was thrown. Not Sarah. She looked as if she were posing for the Mannequin Challenge, which had become so popular earlier that year.

Cassie's dad didn't try to groove one for her, instead pitching her the same as he'd pitched everybody else. Up and in, low and away. Finally the count was two and two. Allie's dad was calling balls and strikes from behind Jack. Sarah had taken all four pitches. If Mr. Bennett had stayed in sequence, the fifth pitch would have been high and inside. It was inside, but it wasn't high enough.

Sarah crushed it to right.

Teddy, who played catcher on the boys' team, could see right away how hard it had been hit, and how deep. Or maybe *hear* how hard it had been hit. But he stumbled slightly as he turned, got his balance back, running for the fence, having picked up the ball again.

Then he stopped, knowing he had no chance, knowing it was gone. He watched the way they all did as the ball disappeared over the fence, clearing it by a lot.

Cassie had been running all the way, with two outs, but she was following the ball, too, as she rounded third. She knew it was a home run about the same time Teddy Madden did.

She trotted the rest of the way home, right arm in the air. Her arm was still in the air as she crossed the plate, so it was easy for Jack to high-five her. The rest of the girls on Cassie's team were treating it exactly like what it was, a walk-off homer. They were jumping up and down next to home plate while they waited for Sarah to finish rounding the bases.

Her head down, as usual.

Cassie wanted to be the first to congratulate her, so she had positioned herself a few feet up the third baseline, in foul territory, waiting.

When Sarah got to her, Cassie couldn't help herself, shouting, "Sarah, that was *awesome*," before she extended both hands toward Sarah, waiting for a double high five.

Sarah didn't high-five Cassie back.

But she did shout back.

"Get off me!"

Then Sarah shoved Cassie, hard, shoved her to the ground, before touching home plate, pivoting, running past the pitcher's mound, past Cassie's dad, for the outfield, as if the rest of her teammates were chasing her.

SIX

Cassie kept telling everybody she was fine, she didn't need to be helped to her feet, it was over, nothing to see here, move along. If one more teammate asked if she was all right, Cassie felt like she was going to be the one yelling for all of them to get off her.

At least Jack knew enough to back off and leave her alone. He just went and stood by himself, over near the bench on the third-base side of the field.

When Cassie walked over to him, she saw that he was smiling.

"That was different," he said.

"You think?" she said.

Cassie didn't realize that Kathleen was right behind her. "How do you like her now?" Kathleen said.

Cassie turned and gave her the Look. "Not in the mood for this right now, Kath," she said. "Not even close."

"I'm sorry," Kathleen said. "Did *I* do something?"

Cassie ignored her, turning instead to face the outfield, where her dad was talking to Sarah, who was standing in her usual spot, head down, of course. Neither one of them seemed in any hurry to join the rest of the team. To Cassie, it already seemed like an hour ago that everybody had been happy and celebrating.

When Cassie was sure it was just her and Jack, she said, "It was my fault."

"It was nobody's fault, Cass," Jack said. "It just happened. Sometimes the heat of the moment gets really, really hot."

"It was because I got up in her face," Cassie said.

"Right," Jack said. "And then you had the nerve to hit *her hands* with *your* chest."

"You know what I mean."

"And you know what I mean. That there was no way you could have known that she was going to react like that."

MIKE LUPICA

"Still should have known better."

"Are you insane?" Jack said. "You haven't even known her for a whole week. You were supposed to know she'd go off because you congratulated her for hitting a home run?"

"I've been reading up a lot on Asperger's," Cassie said. "I'm telling you, I should have been smarter."

"Yeah," Jack said, "in a week you're an expert."

"You were right there," Cassie said. "She was fine until I yelled."

"Okay," Jack said. "I'll give you that. And next time you won't."

"She must feel terrible," Cassie said, staring again at the outfield, where her dad and Sarah hadn't moved.

"You're already one of the smartest people I know," Jack said. "But you need to leave this alone right now. Because you have no idea *what* she's feeling."

"I should go talk to her."

"Your *dad* is talking to her."

"I don't want this to be a thing."

"It's already a thing!" Jack said. "That's why you need to let your dad handle it."

"I like to handle things for myself."

"Wow," Jack said, "I hadn't ever picked up on that."

Cassie didn't have her phone in the pocket of her shorts. She didn't know what time it was, or what time the scrimmage had ended, or how long her dad and Sarah had been out there. But it had been a while.

Jack touched Cassie on the shoulder and pointed across the diamond. Sarah's parents had shown up now with some of the other parents, meaning it was seven o'clock, and time for pickup. The Milligans saw what everybody could see: the rest of the Red Sox players milling around at home plate still, or collecting their stuff at the first-base bench, or the fence behind it. And there was Sarah with Cassie's dad, out in center. Sarah's parents had to know something had happened. Not exactly what. But something.

"I should go explain to them what happened," Cassie said.

But before she could even take one step in their direction, Jack gently placed a hand on her arm.

"Let the grown-ups handle this," he said.

"You're saying I can't?"

"Not as well as the grown-ups," Jack said. "Not even you."

Mr. and Mrs. Milligan walked to the outfield. When they got there, Cassie saw her dad speak to them. She saw Mr. Milligan nodding his head. She thought he might even be smiling. Mrs. Milligan put an arm around Sarah's shoulders. With her other hand she put a finger under Sarah's chin, finally making her look up.

After a few more minutes they all started walking toward the infield, Mrs. Milligan's arm still around Sarah's shoulders. They turned at second base and walked across the infield dirt toward first. Mrs. Milligan stayed with Sarah. Mr. Milligan walked over and collected Sarah's bat bag, either recognizing it right away or knowing exactly where it would be.

Then he and Mrs. Milligan and Sarah were opening the door in the fence and walking through it, heading for the parking lot.

Before Jack could stop her this time, Cassie was jogging after them.

They were in the parking lot when she caught up with them.

"Sarah," Cassie said. "Hey, Sarah."

She was careful not to raise her voice.

Sarah turned around, saw who it was. This time she didn't look away.

"I just wanted to tell you I was sorry," she said. "What happened was my fault."

Sarah didn't say anything, just stared at her, without expression. She didn't seem angry now. She didn't seem anything.

"I shouldn't have gotten up on you that way," Cassie said. "It won't happen again."

Still nothing from Sarah.

"Okay?" Cassie said.

Finally, in a voice that Cassie could barely hear, Sarah Milligan said, "Please stop talking."

"I'm not trying to bother you."

"Please stop talking, please stop talking, please stop talking," Sarah said.

So Cassie did.

"Stop talking," Sarah said again.

Then she opened the door and got into the backseat of the car. At some point Mr. Milligan must have handed Sarah her glove. Cassie was close enough to the car to look through the window and see that Sarah was wearing it now, pounding it again and again with her right fist, like she was trying to break it in all over again.

"It really was my fault," Cassie said to Mr. and Mrs. Milligan.

Mrs. Milligan smiled, but her face looked sad.

"You couldn't possibly have known that congratulating Sarah would make her act that way," she said. "Please don't blame yourself. We've had Sarah her whole life. We know her better than anyone. You've only known her since tryouts."

"I want to help her," Cassie said, keeping her voice low.

"I'm sure you do, dear," Mrs. Milligan said. "I'm sure you do."

She opened the door and got into the front seat. Mr. Milligan walked around the car and got in on the driver's side. Then Cassie heard the car starting, and watched it slowly pull away.

As it disappeared in the direction of town, Cassie found herself feeling the way she had with Peter Rizzo, the autistic boy who'd been in the fifth grade with her.

Somehow she was going to fix this.

They were at Fierro's now, their usual booth in the back, Jack and Gus on one side of the table, Cassie and Teddy on the other. By the time they'd gotten there, Greta and Kathleen and Nell had been across the room in a booth of their own.

After Cassie and the guys ordered, Greta came over and said, "This wasn't even a real game, and now I'm wondering if every game is going to be like this."

She pointed over at her table and said, "Everybody's worried."

"It'll be fine," Cassie said.

"And you know that . . . *how?*"

"We'll all just have to figure it out," Cassie said. "Sarah included. She lost her head because I lost mine."

"Yeah," Greta said. "You gave her a big shout-out for hitting a home run. What were you thinking?"

"But at least it all started because she *did* hit that home run," Cassie said. "I've never hit a ball that far."

Cassie didn't want to be talking about this with Greta. She wanted to talk about it with Jack and Gus and Teddy. But it wasn't as if she could get up and leave her own booth.

And Greta wasn't finished.

"Just because you want to be friends with her doesn't mean we have to be friends with her," she said. "And just because you're okay with her being on our team doesn't mean we are."

"Just because I'm trying to be nice to her doesn't mean that we're friends," Cassie said, voice rising, unable to stop it. She knew she was tired, and knew she was getting crankier with Greta Zahn by the second. "Do you see her sitting here with me? I just want this to work out for her, and work out for us. Are you okay with *that*?"

"Our team doesn't need any help, and you know it," Greta said.

Then she was the one who walked away.

When she was out of earshot, Teddy said, "Forget about being friends with the new girl. Why did you ever want to be friends with *her*?"

"Good question," Cassie said. "We've never had much in common other than softball."

"Usually that's enough for you," Gus said.

"I keep reminding myself of that," Cassie said.

Their pizza came. They all ate in silence for a few minutes, Cassie going through the motions, because she'd lost her appetite. A couple of times she looked across at her teammates. One time when she did, they all stopped talking.

"It *is* gonna be fine, right?" Cassie said. "We all just have to get used to Sarah. Me included. It'll be fine."

She knew how much she sounded as if she were trying to talk herself into something.

Jack leaned forward a little and said, "But what if it's not?"

"Hey," Cassie said. "Whose side are you on?"

"Yours," he said. "Like always. But you know what a bear you are for winning. In anything. You just gotta know that it's not only your own team you have to worry about. There's gonna be another team on the field."

It stopped her. "I hadn't even thought about that," she said.

"Not saying they're gonna be mean," he said. "But it's not like they'll be worried about making softball the positive experience for Sarah that you want it to be. They'll just be looking to knock off the best team in the league. Maybe in the state."

Teddy asked Cassie then what her dad had said after Sarah and her parents were gone. Cassie told them what her dad had told her: that what had happened tonight would happen from time to time, unexpectedly. When Sarah was younger, she'd experienced some bullying in school, and it had made her more sensitive and sometimes defensive than she already was, even though there hadn't been any bullying for a long time in Sarah's life, at least that they knew about. But she still had her guard up, constantly, for aggressive behavior of any kind. And Mr.

and Mrs. Milligan had told Cassie's dad that the other kids on the Red Sox were going to have to understand that what they considered normal communication might not be normal for a child with Asperger's.

"Dad said that we need to have *our* guard up, especially when it comes to our body language and facial expressions," she said.

She pushed her plate to the middle of the table, having only eaten a couple of bites, and lowered her voice.

"Don't any of you repeat this," Cassie said. "But maybe it is too much, having her on the team."

"Won't repeat it," Teddy said, "because we all know you don't mean it."

"But Greta's right about something, as much as I hate admitting that," she said. "We *don't* need her to be great."

"But won't it be greater if you're great with her?" Gus said. Then he grinned and nodded at her plate and said, "Don't mean to change the subject, but do you mind if I finish that?"

Cassie couldn't help it. She smiled. "Good that all this stress hasn't made you lose your appetite."

"I need to keep my strength up to be a good wingman," he said.

Cassie nodded her head toward Greta and Kathleen and Nell.

"Isn't that supposed to be *their* job too?" she said.

MIKE LUPICA

In anything.

Maybe, she thought, lying on her bed after dinner and waiting for the Milligans to show up, it went back to something her grandmother—her dad's mom—had told her not long before she'd died. The beautiful old woman whose name was Connie but whom Cassie had always called "Nonnie" from the time she'd mispronounced it as a little girl spent most of the last few months of her life in her bed, suffering from emphysema. But Cassie would sit there with her for hours and just talk to her. Mostly Cassie just listened. Until the end her grandmother, who'd read as much as anyone else Cassie had ever known, had a stack of books on the dresser next to her bed. One day one of them was *The Great Gatsby*, which Nonnie said she'd first read more than sixty years before.

"I'm going to give you a piece of advice that Nick Carraway's father gave him in this book," Nonnie said to Cassie. "Not everybody in this life has had the advantages you've had already."

Cassie said that she wasn't sure she understood, and her grandmother said, "Of all the talents God has given you, make sure the one you use the most is kindness."

Cassie promised her she would try. And Cassie wished she had tried harder with Peter Rizzo. Sometimes she wished the whole world was like one of her favorite TV shows, *Speechless*, in which the best character, and the funniest, was a boy suffering

"None of this is supposed to feel like a job," Jack said.

"Then how come it's starting to feel like that already?" she said.

They decided not to walk up the street and get ice cream. Teddy texted his mom, who was picking them up, and told her they'd finished eating. On her way out Cassie stopped at her teammates' table, smiling a smile she really didn't feel, and said, "C'mon, you guys. There must have been times when one of you wanted to give me a good shove."

Kathleen smiled up at her. "You mean like now?" she said.

Cassie forced a laugh out of herself, thinking, *Yeah, big joke*. But she was the only one who laughed. Only when she was in the front room at Fierro's did she hear a big shout of laughter from them.

She didn't turn around. It had been a long enough night already. She hoped it wasn't the beginning of a long season.

All of a sudden Sarah wasn't the only one on the team who seemed alone.

SEVEN

Sarah and her parents were coming over to Cassie's house the next night after dinner.

It gave Cassie some time to think about everything that had happened to the team so far, and also to ask herself why it was so important to her to have things work out with Sarah.

She kept coming back to the autistic boy in fifth grade, Peter Rizzo.

She had never been one of the kids, boys or girls, who had made fun of him behind his back. It had only been a handful of them, and they never did it to the boy's face. Looking back on it now, Cassie didn't even think they were being malicious. They were ten-year-olds, and were acting like ten-year olds.

None of Cassie's friends, at least none that she knew about, had an autistic brother or sister. For most of the kids in the fifth grade, it was likely that this was the first time they'd ever been around an autistic boy or girl. So no one was sure how to act. Maybe some of them were just acting the way they usually did, about almost everything, thinking they were being funny when they weren't.

But what Cassie did know is that she had never told anybody to stop when they *were* making fun of Peter Rizzo. She definitely knew that. And she definitely knew, in her heart, the one her dad said he knew so well, that she hadn't made enough of an effort to make things easier on Peter, whether she could have done that or not. Oh, she told herself she wanted to fix things. To her that meant making Peter feel more welcome in the classes they shared, and in their grade. But when he left after the school year ended, she was honest enough with herself to know that she hadn't done enough. It had bothered her ever since. It wasn't just that she'd let this boy down. She felt as if she'd let herself down.

She *hated* letting herself down.

from cerebral palsy. Except, Cassie knew, that wasn't even the best way to describe it. The character, JJ, didn't act as if he were suffering at all. He just got on with things, often using humor like it was his greatest talent, being friends with whom he wanted, mostly with a friendly groundskeeper at his school.

Maybe that's who I should try to be like with Sarah, Cassie thought. *A friendly groundskeeper.*

It just wasn't working out that way so far. Maybe tonight could be a way to start over.

"Don't force it," her mom had said at dinner. "Just let it happen."

"Not forcing things, Mom?" Cassie had said. "Not exactly my strong suit."

"Well, honey, there's a first time for everything, isn't there?"

Mrs. Milligan's first name was Kari. "With a *K*," she said. "Rhymes with 'car.'" Mr. Milligan's first name was Jim. They all went and sat in the living room.

Let it happen, Cassie reminded herself.

Sarah sat between her parents on the couch. She didn't have her head down tonight, maybe because she had her parents with her. Her eyes, Cassie saw, kept moving from Cassie to Cassie's parents, almost as if she were waiting to see which one of them would make the first move.

But it was Sarah's mom who spoke first.

"Sarah would like to apologize to you, Cassie, for what happened yesterday," she said.

"She doesn't have to, really," Cassie said.

"Yes, Cassie, she does." Her manner was friendly and firm at the same time. It was as if she were letting Cassie know who was in charge, at least for the moment.

"Sorry," Sarah said.

"Sorry for what?" Mrs. Milligan said.

Cassie still heard the same tone from her, friendly but firm.

"I'm sorry for shoving you," Sarah said.

Now she put her head down.

Cassie was standing in front of the fireplace. There was a lot she wanted to say. But she knew this wasn't about her right now. So all she said was, "I accept your apology, Sarah. I don't want us to just be teammates. I want us to be friends."

Sarah didn't respond, just clasped her hands in her lap and kept staring at the floor.

"Okay," Sarah said.

Then everybody was silent for what seemed like an awkwardly long time, until Cassie couldn't take it anymore and said, "Sarah?"

Sarah looked up.

"Would you like to see my room?" Cassie said.

For a second Cassie thought she saw fear in Sarah's eyes, or maybe uncertainty, as if she hadn't signed up for anything other than the apology, maybe thinking that as soon as she had apologized that she and her parents could leave.

"Why don't you?" Sarah's dad said. "While the grown-ups get to know one another a little better, you and Cassie can do the same."

Sarah turned to look at her dad, then turned back to her mom, as if one of them would change their mind. But they both just smiled at her until Sarah said, "Okay, I guess."

"Follow me," Cassie said.

"Okay, I guess."

She didn't sound okay, but she followed Cassie out of the living room.

At least, Cassie thought, *I cleaned my room today, so the mess won't make her even more afraid.* But once they were in there, Sarah just stood next to the door, as if so she could make a fast getaway if she needed to.

"Why don't you just grab the chair next to my desk," Cassie said.

Sarah hesitated slightly, walked quickly to the chair, sat down, clasped her hands back together in her lap.

Cassie hopped onto the bed and sat facing Sarah, cross-legged.

"My room's not usually nearly this neat," Cassie said, "not gonna lie."

There was no response.

"I'm usually kind of a slob," Cassie said. "How about you?"

Sarah didn't respond to that, either, and Cassie was starting to wonder how many more inane comments she was going to have to make, when Sarah blurted out, "You don't have to be my friend!"

Cassie was the one startled by a loud noise.

"I know I don't," she said, keeping her own voice low. "I don't think I *have* to. I *want* to."

Sarah was staring down again, clenching and unclenching her hands now.

"You don't know anything about me," she said.

"But I'd like to."

Now Sarah picked up her head, her eyes intensely focused on Cassie, almost fiercely.

"Why?" she said.

The question stopped her, and not just because she had no answer for Sarah. It was because Cassie had never asked that question of herself. Cassie realized in that moment that she had never spent much time, or any time, looking at things from Sarah's point of view, or trying to understand why Sarah might be suspicious of someone she hardly knew suddenly trying to act like her guardian angel.

As serious as Sarah was, Cassie couldn't keep herself from smiling.

"You got me."

"What does that mean?"

"It means I can't explain why."

For the first time, Sarah smiled back at her.

It wasn't like an episode of *Speechless*, or any other television show that Cassie watched. They didn't work everything out in the next half hour. They weren't friends by the time Sarah's parents called her from downstairs and told her it was time to go.

The conversation between them didn't get a whole lot easier, but Cassie was fine with that. She'd stopped thinking that any of this was going to be easy. Her parents always told her that the things that made you work the most meant the most.

They talked about basketball, because Sarah had played basketball before she'd played softball. Sarah asked Cassie if she played basketball. Cassie said she did.

"I even played on a boys' team last season," Cassie told her.

Sarah's eyes got big. "They let you do that?"

"They kind of didn't have a choice," Cassie said. "If you're good enough at something, nobody should be able to hold you back."

Sarah frowned and said, "But why did you want to?"

"I guess to show people I really was good enough."

Sarah was still frowning. "Did people treat you differently?"

"Yeah," Cassie said. "Yeah, they did."

"Was it worth it?"

It was a question Cassie had asked herself all season long and was still asking herself, even though the Warriors had won the league championship, and she'd played a big part in their doing that.

"It was worth it," she said finally.

"Why was it worth it?"

Cassie said, "At first I thought it was just proving a point to the other boys. But it ended up being about me proving something to myself."

"On my team," Sarah said, "I guess . . . I guess I proved something."

"That you were better than they first thought you were?"

"I guess."

They were still talking, Cassie and the girl who had complained about people talking, a girl who paused before she said something and then spoke slowly when she did, as if somehow weighing every word, or afraid she might be about to use the wrong one.

"Even though I was on a team, and even though I pride

myself on being a team player," Cassie said, "I was also playing for myself."

"I never thought about it that way," Sarah said.

"It's about having pride in yourself," Cassie said.

Sarah nodded. "I guess."

Sarah's mom called her then. Sarah jumped out of the chair, and walked out of the room ahead of Cassie, and down the stairs without saying a word.

Good talk, Cassie wanted to say, but didn't.

She just said good night to Mr. and Mrs. Milligan and said she'd see Sarah at the Red Sox opening game on Saturday.

"Same," Sarah said over her shoulder, already walking quickly toward their car.

When the Milligans were all in the car, Cassie's mom said, "Well, did you learn anything tonight?"

"I did, actually."

"Care to share?"

"Maybe Sarah and I aren't as different as I thought," Cassie said.

Cassie wasn't getting carried away by tonight. But maybe this was a new beginning for her and Sarah, with the season about to officially begin on Saturday.

It definitely beat a good, hard shove to the chest anytime.

EIGHT

The opener was against the Hollis Hills Yankees at Highland Park. The weather in Walton was so perfect on Saturday that Cassie thought it would have been a crime not to be playing softball today.

In the morning Cassie called Jack and asked if he and Teddy and Gus were coming to the game.

Jack laughed. "Is that what we'd call in English class a rhetorical question?" Then he said of course they were coming, their practice at Walton Middle in the morning with their All-Star team, the Cubs, would be over by ten o'clock, and Cassie's game wasn't until eleven.

"I'm actually glad you've got a game, especially for Teddy and Gus," he said. "It'll take their minds off all the drama we're having now with *our* team."

Neither Teddy nor Gus liked their new coach. His name was Ken Anthony, and he was new to Walton this year, along with his son, Sam, who was expected to be one of the Cubs' star pitchers. Sam didn't go to Walton Middle. He was actually attending Hollis Academy, the private school in town. But because his family lived in Walton, he was eligible to play for the Cubs. And his dad had been asked to coach the team. Ken Anthony had been a minor-league pitcher before a shoulder injury ended his career. But according to Jack, it was clear that Coach Anthony thought his son was going to be the one in the family who *did* make it to the big leagues.

That wasn't the problem they were having with their new coach, though. The problem was that Mr. Anthony acted as if he were managing the real Cubs. He was loud, for one thing. Teddy said that not only did the guy act as if he'd invented baseball, he treated summer baseball as if it were military school, actually making them drop and do push-ups if they threw to the wrong base, or made a mistake on the bases.

TEAM PLAYERS

"So he hasn't lightened up?" Cassie said.

"I don't think he's going to lighten up," Jack said. "It doesn't make me as crazy as it does the other guys. I just sort of try to tune him out. But Teddy and Gus aren't having any fun. Teddy's even talked about quitting, and I don't think he's joking."

"All this drama on both our teams," Cassie said, "and neither one of us plays a real game until today."

"We'll be there," Jack said. "And, Cass? Good luck."

"Hope I don't need much."

"You pitching?"

"Look at you," she said, "with another rhetorical question!"

As soon as she got to the field, she could feel the excitement inside her. And even after what had happened at Fierro's the other day, she could see that Greta and Kathleen and Allie and the rest of her teammates were just as excited. Maybe they'd all figured that if any one of them did well, they all did well. You didn't have to like all of your teammates. It didn't change the fact that you were all in it together. Cassie knew it would probably sound lame if she actually said that to them. But she honestly believed it.

Nothing that had been said about Sarah at Fierro's mattered today. Nothing that had happened at the end of that scrimmage mattered. The game mattered. Beating the Hollis Hills Yankees mattered today. Everything else was just noise.

MIKE LUPICA

She sought out Greta and Kathleen after they'd finished batting practice and infield practice, and bumped fists with both of them.

"We are *not* losing this game," Cassie said.

"We're not losing *any* games," Greta said.

"Well, you know what they say," Cassie said. "We can't win them all if we don't win today."

Kathleen smiled at her, as if things were the same as they used to be between them. "Just hope our starting pitcher still has it," she said.

"Are you serious?" Cassie said. "Have you seen that Cassie Bennett pitch? I *love* her."

"Tell us about it," Greta said. But she was smiling too.

From the time Sarah arrived at the field, there was just something about her body language that made it seem as if she were keeping even more distance from her teammates than usual. Something that told *Cassie* to keep her distance. Sarah looked more anxious than she had at tryouts, more locked in to her routines. She set her bat bag in the same place she always did under the bench. She stood in her spot in the outfield during batting practice. Cassie's dad made sure that everybody hit in the same order during BP as they had at the last couple of practices, the same batting order he was going to use in the game. Cassie was ahead of Sarah, with Brooke Connors behind her.

With every pitch Sarah saw during BP, she went through all of her rituals, pulling at the shoulders of the blue Red Sox T-shirt with the red trim, tapping home plate, all of it.

All Cassie said to her, right before the game started, was "Good luck today."

"Good luck today," Sarah said back, and then went and sat at the end of the bench, glove already on her hand, waiting for Mr. Bennett to give them the signal to take the field for the top of the first. It was as if Sarah's visit the other night hadn't happened. She didn't mention it. Neither did Cassie.

"You think Sarah's gonna be okay today?" Cassie said to her dad.

"We're about to find out," he said. "But just so you know? Okay would be perfectly okay with me."

"Okay, then!" Cassie said, and gave her dad a high five.

She turned then and saw Jack and Teddy and Gus, standing at the fence behind the Red Sox bench, waving her over.

"Well, you know what they say," Jack said when Cassie got with them. "You're only as good as your starting pitcher."

"Yup," Teddy said, "that's what they say, isn't that right, Gus?"

"That's what they say," Gus said, grinning at Cassie.

"All of you," Cassie said, "please shut up."

Jack put out his hand. Cassie put hers on top of it. Teddy and Gus put theirs on top of hers.

MIKE LUPICA

"Your team is the same as our team," Jack said.

Cassie looked at him, and smiled. "I know that," she said. "The home team."

Gus said, "You are aware that you won't have Jack or me to pass the ball to today, right?"

"I'll try to manage," she said.

"How we lookin' with the new girl?" Gus said.

Cassie told him that it was the same as always. They were about to play the game and find out.

Cassie knew she was going to be on the same strict pitch count she'd been under last season. Eighty was the magic number. Her dad might let her go a couple of pitches past that, but just a couple and no more. He said that all young pitchers' arms had to be protected, whether it was a Little League boy throwing overhand or his daughter whipping the ball in underhand.

Chris Bennett had shown Cassie the schedule. Teams in their league were going to play two games a week. The plan was for Cassie to pitch every other game. Brooke was the next best pitcher on their team, so she was going to be the team's other starter. Allie was going to be their closer. Cassie's dad had told her that once they got into the season, he wanted to give Sarah a shot too. But that was for later. He said he didn't want to put too much on her plate too soon.

"It's not just Sarah," he'd told Cassie. "My job as a coach is to make sure every player on our team is in her comfort zone."

Cassie was the one in the zone today, and making the Hollis Hills hitters extremely *un*comfortable. She felt that good on the mound, almost as if she'd come from last year's championship game to this game. By the time she was through the top of the second, she'd struck out five of the first six batters she'd faced. When the Red Sox were all back at the bench after the top of the second, her catcher, Brooke, said, "You know what the sound of the ball in my mitt is? Like my favorite song."

But the Yankees' starting pitcher, Sydney Ellis, was already pitching as if she wanted to match Cassie strikeout for strikeout. By the end of the fourth, the game was still 0–0. Each team had just one hit. Cassie got the first for her team with two outs in the bottom of the fourth, a double over first base and down the right-field line with one out. Sarah, who'd struck out her first time up, clearly nervous, came up behind Cassie and hit the ball really well, but the Yankees' center fielder chased it down about six feet short of the fence. Cassie tagged up and went to second, getting herself into scoring position, but Brooke lined out to left, and the game stayed scoreless.

The only ball hit to Sarah so far had been a single to center by Sydney Ellis. There'd been no fly balls hit her way, no chance for her to show off either her speed or her arm. But Cassie wasn't really fixed on what Sarah was doing. She was just in the game she was pitching, and the game they were *all* playing. You could try to practice the way you played as much as you wanted. But you couldn't fool yourself. Real games were different. They just were. Even on the same field you practiced on, it was as if you were breathing different air. It was, Cassie knew, the rarefied air of competition, of doing something you loved, doing it as well as you could, your best against their best. Didn't matter whether it was the first game or the last game, especially if you were pitching. It always came down to this:

Here it comes.

See if you can hit it.

The best part for her, once she got through the top of the fifth with another strikeout and a couple of weak ground balls, was that her pitch count was low.

"One more inning," her dad said after she'd struck out Sydney Ellis to end the Yankees' fifth. "You're sitting on seventy pitches, and it's only our first game."

Cassie knew better than to debate him. She knew he was right about pitchers' arms, and knew he was looking out for her.

"A deal is a deal," she said.

"You're the one who's dealing today," he said.

"All I need now is a run," Cassie said.

The Red Sox didn't get it in the bottom of the fifth, because

Sydney was still dealing, setting down the Red Sox in order, two strikeouts, a foul pop-up to the first baseman.

Cassie knew she only had ten pitches, maybe a couple more, if she wanted to finish one more half inning. She stepped on it then with her fastball, doing the things the announcers always talked about pitchers doing when she'd watch a game on television: reaching back for a little extra. She struck out the first two batters in the sixth on six pitches, before going to 1–2 on the next girl up, the Yankees' shortstop. She was sitting on seventy-nine pitches. Before she threw the next pitch, she managed to briefly catch her dad's eye.

And wink.

Then she blew strike three past the shortstop, whom she'd heard the Yankees call Kendall. Big swing, much bigger miss, at a high fastball. Game still scoreless. Cassie knew she was a shortstop now, and that Allie was coming in to pitch the seventh. Ana Rivera would move from shortstop and replace Allie at second base.

They still needed a run, and almost got it in the bottom of the sixth. Greta singled with two outs. Cassie ripped a single to left behind her. First and second. Sarah was at the plate now, in a hero spot, a chance to knock in what might be the winning run in the first official softball game of her life.

It was also a chance for her to win over some skeptical

teammates, show them she belonged and convince them that she did.

Cassie watched from first base as Sarah went through her routine. She didn't look out at Sydney, still in there for Hollis Hills, until Sarah had gone through all her checks and tugs and little rituals, like she was checking off one box after another in her mind. And today Cassie had noticed she was doing one more thing: once she was in the batter's box, she gave a quick look up into the bleachers behind the Red Sox bench to where her parents were sitting, and mouthed something. Cassie wasn't a good enough lip-reader to know what.

Sarah didn't take any pitches this time, something she had done her first two times up, passing up two right down the middle. Cassie had started to wonder if that was part of her routine too.

Not this time.

This time she swung at the first pitch she saw, and connected. Big-time. When Cassie heard the sound of the ball coming off Sarah's aluminum bat, saw the flight of it over her head as she was flying toward second base, running all the way with two outs, she thought it looked exactly the same as the home run Sarah had hit to right to win the scrimmage.

From the time Cassie had started playing softball, she'd heard all the jokes about how you always put your worst fielder in right field. Only, there weren't any worst fielders in All-Stars, and certainly not on the Yankees, whose right fielder had already made two dazzling plays, one a diving catch on a ball in front of her, the other on the backhand as she'd run into the gap in right-center to catch up with a ball Brooke had hit.

The catch she made now was better than both of them. The girl—Cassie would find out her name was Marcie Kincaid when she sought her out to congratulate her after the game—somehow caught up with a ball that had been hit directly over her head, a step from the wall. She reached up at the last moment, made another backhand catch. She put out her free hand to stop herself from running into the wall, or maybe through it, turned around, and showed everybody that the ball was still in her glove, while sprinting back toward the infield.

The game was still 0–0.

Sarah had come that close to a home run. Even if it hadn't been a home run, the Red Sox had come that close to scoring two runs if the ball had just managed to get over Marcie Kincaid's head. For now Marcie had saved the game for her team.

"Well," Cassie said to Brooke when she jogged back to their bench, "*that* was aggressive."

So now it was the top of the last, if one team could find a way to scratch out a run. If the game stayed 0–0, they would get just one extra inning to break the tie. Or it would end in a tie. That was the rule in All-Stars.

Nobody wanted a tie, not after a game like this.

Allie did the one thing you never wanted to do in the late innings of a close game: walked the leadoff hitter. Cassie could see how nervous she was, even though she'd been their closer last season too. Allie had the arm, anybody could see that. But suddenly she was acting as if she were outside her comfort zone, and outside the strike zone, as she tried to keep the game at 0–0, tried not to give up the run that might lose a lot of her teammates the first game they'd lost in two years.

She struck out the next batter. But gave up a single to Marcie Kincaid. First and second, one out.

She got another strikeout.

But then she walked the Yankees' third baseman, loading the bases for Sydney Ellis, who had hit the ball hard every single time she'd come up against Cassie, even though she just had one base hit to show for it.

Allie had to be careful with her, obviously, just not too careful, or she risked walking in the go-ahead run and leaving them loaded.

Cassie called time and ran into the mound from shortstop, big smile on her face. She took the ball out of Allie's glove and rubbed it up.

"You got this, girlfriend," she said.

In a low voice Allie said, "No, *you'd* have this."

Cassie kept her own voice low now. "If you're gonna miss with her, miss inside. Trust me, you don't want this girl to extend her arms."

She put the ball back, hard, into Allie's glove.

"These are the fun parts," Cassie said.

Allie managed a small smile. "Thanks for reminding me."

The count went to 2–2. Both of Allie's misses *had* been inside. Now she put another fastball on the inside corner, the best pitch she'd thrown yet. Sydney took a big swing, and got her bat on the ball, but it sounded to Cassie as if she'd caught it closer to the handle, not getting all of it. Sydney had gotten enough to hit the ball between Kathleen and Sarah in left-center field.

From the night of tryouts, Cassie's dad had been clear about something in outfield drills:

He wanted his center fielder to take charge on balls like this, like his center fielder was the quarterback of the outfielders, calling the plays, and calling for the ball.

Cassie could only turn and follow the flight of the ball, knowing there was nothing to do about the two base runners behind her. They were doing what she'd done on the ball Sarah had hit in the bottom of the sixth, running all the way with two outs.

She did hear Ana call out to her from second, "You take the cutoff if there is one," both of them hoping there wasn't going to be a cutoff throw, that either Kathleen or Sarah was going to make the catch.

If somebody made the call in the outfield, they made it as Ana had yelled over to Cassie.

The next thing Cassie saw was Sarah Milligan coming to a dead stop and Kathleen reaching in vain as the ball fell between them, and rolled all the way to the wall.

When it finally stopped rolling, Sydney was standing on third and it was 3–0 for the Yankees. Technically the game wasn't over yet.

But everybody on the Red Sox knew it was.

NINE

The Red Sox got two runners on in the bottom of the seventh, to at least give themselves a chance to come all the way back. But Kathleen made the last out of the game, a routine fly ball to center.

For the first time since the summer after sixth grade, Cassie's softball team had lost. She'd forgotten what that felt like. She had known she wasn't going to keep winning games for as long as she played. As loaded as their team was, she hadn't really thought they were going to win out again this summer. They'd all heard about how strong some of the other teams in All-Stars were.

It didn't mean she had to like the feeling.

Her dad did what he always did after games, after they'd all shaken hands with the players on the other team: he gathered his own players around him in short right field. No parents. Just the team.

When all the players were out there, Chris Bennett had to walk back to the bench, where Sarah was seated, and ask her to come join them.

The other players were seated in the grass, in a circle. Sarah stood behind them.

"Well, that was some great game with a not-so-great ending," Chris Bennett said. "But you'll get tired of hearing me say this by the time our season is over. People always remember what happens at the end of a close game. But it's never just one thing, even when it looks like it is. Sports is way more complicated than that. We had our chances today. And when we get those same type of chances on Tuesday night, we'll convert enough of them to win the game."

Tuesday night was their next game, against Moran.

Sarah was across from where Cassie was sitting. She wasn't looking down. She seemed to be looking past Cassie and past the outfield fences, her eyes fixed on some distant point. Or maybe on nothing at all.

Cassie's dad smacked his hands together. "So, we good?" he asked.

"No," Kathleen said. "We're not."

It was like she couldn't control herself any longer, couldn't hold in everything she'd been holding in since she'd made the last out. Or maybe since Sydney's ball had fallen between her and Sarah.

She got up now, and turned to face Sarah Milligan, who was still staring off, now shifting her weight quickly from one foot to the other.

"That was your ball," Kathleen said to Sarah.

Sarah wasn't looking at her.

"I'm talking to you, Sarah," Kathleen said.

But Sarah didn't look at Kathleen right away. She looked at Cassie, as if somehow Cassie could do something to help her.

As if Cassie could fix this.

Cassie's dad said, "Not the time, Kath."

"What would be a good time to say what we're all thinking, Coach Bennett?" Kathleen said. "You always tell us that the center fielder is the one who's supposed to take charge. It was her ball, and she knows it."

Sarah spoke now, in a voice that Cassie could barely hear,

one she wondered if Kathleen could hear, and Kathleen was standing right in front of Sarah by now.

But Sarah was looking back at Cassie.

"She said it was hers," Sarah said.

"*I did not!*" Kathleen said, in a voice that Cassie knew was much too loud for Sarah. Cassie was worried it would spook Sarah and make her do something now with Kathleen that Sarah would regret. Like what she'd done to Cassie.

But she stood her ground as Kathleen said, "*I did not call you off!*"

Sarah was still looking at Cassie, as if Cassie in that moment was the one friend on the team she had. And maybe Cassie was.

"She said, 'Mine,'" Sarah said. "That's why I stopped."

Kathleen said, "That's a lie."

Now Sarah said, "Yes you did, yes you did, yes you did," her words all running together.

"Girls," Cassie's dad, trying to keep his own voice calm, "this needs to end."

"You mean until she loses us our next game?" Kathleen said. "She's the one who called 'mine.'"

Then why, Cassie thought, *did Kathleen keep running?*

"I didn't say anything," Kathleen said.

Now Sarah Milligan was the one yelling, and starting to cry at the same time.

TEAM PLAYERS

"YES YOU DID, YES YOU DID, YES YOU DID!"

She couldn't stop the words from coming out of her this way, the way she couldn't stop the tears from streaming down her face.

"YOU HAVE TO BELIEVE ME!"

She wasn't addressing the whole team now.

Just Cassie.

But when Cassie hesitated just enough, not even knowing what she was supposed to say, not knowing what the right answer was, Sarah was on the run again. She didn't run in the direction of her parents, waiting behind the bench with the other Red Sox parents. She just took off across the outfield at Highland Park, only stopping long enough to open the door in center field. Then she ran again, in the direction of town.

Cassie ran after her.

TEN

Cassie was fast, but Sarah Milligan was faster.

Cassie wasn't sure what Sarah's parents planned to do about their daughter taking off this way, or how concerned they were, or if they'd already gotten into their car. She didn't know if this happened a lot with Sarah. But Cassie wasn't waiting to find out.

Maybe Sarah took off all the time, and always ended up in

the same place. Maybe this was a routine for her too. But Cassie didn't care.

She ran, even though Sarah had a good lead on her.

Sarah crossed the kids' playground at Highland Park, cut across the big field where the Walton High School team played its games, then through the soccer field next to the duck pond. If Sarah had started to get tired, or slow down, Cassie didn't see it, because as far as Cassie could tell, she hadn't made up any ground, and might have lost some.

At their second-to-last practice before the season had started, Sarah had run down another ball that Cassie had thought was uncatchable when Brooke hit it. But when Sarah did catch it, Cassie's dad said, "That girl can run all day."

Cassie hoped that wasn't actually true.

If Cassie could just catch her, she could tell Sarah what she should have told her on the field, even in front of their teammates:

That she believed her.

Sarah was running in the direction of downtown Walton.

When she got there, she finally stopped, as if she weren't sure where she wanted to go next.

She had run past the bookstore, and Rosie's Café, and Fierro's, and Cold Stone. By the time she did stop in front of a clothing store called Family Britches, Cassie was a block behind, but didn't call out to her. Cassie had never seen Sarah look back, so she couldn't know that Cassie had been chasing her since Highland Park. But Cassie was afraid that if she did call Sarah's name, the girl might just take off again.

Sarah had her hands on her hips, staring across Main Street, as if she were deciding where she was headed next. Or maybe she was the one who'd finally gotten tired, and was just catching her breath.

Cassie stopped running, getting her own breath under control, until she was a few feet behind her.

She made sure to keep her voice under control too.

"Sarah," she said.

Sarah wheeled around, eyes wide, and Cassie really was afraid she might bolt all over again. But before she could, Cassie smiled at her and said, "Please don't make me chase you again."

"What do you want?"

"To talk to you."

"Why?" Sarah said. "Nobody believes me."

"I do," Cassie said.

Sarah frowned. "Then why didn't you say so back at the field?"

"I didn't get the chance before you turned into Usain Bolt."

"I'm not lying."

"I know."

"How do you know?"

"Because you were the one who stopped and she was the one who kept running," Cassie said. "If you called her off the ball, it should have been the other way around."

"*I know,*" Sarah said, almost as if she were in pain.

Cassie was afraid Sarah might start crying again, and watched now as she took in deep gulps of air as if doing everything she could *not* to cry.

"But what difference does it make?" Sarah said. "Even if you do believe me, nobody else on the team does. And now they're not going to want me on the team more than ever."

She was right, and Cassie knew it. Not all of their teammates were going to think that way. Enough of them were, though.

But Cassie wasn't going to tell that to Sarah.

"We can't do anything about that right this minute," Cassie said. "And a lot of things get said after you lose a game like that."

Actually, Cassie couldn't even remember what it was like to lose a game like that, because it had been so long.

Sarah didn't respond at first, so Cassie kept going. "For now, the first thing we have to do is let your mom and dad know where you are. Do you have your phone with you?"

"It's in my bat bag back at the field."

"Do you know their number?"

Cassie knew it was a dumb comment as soon as she'd made it. Sarah picked right up on it.

"You think I don't?"

"No," Cassie said. "But there's plenty of numbers I don't remember. It's why they invented contacts."

Sarah slowly recited the number.

Cassie had her phone with her, having grabbed it from her own bat bag as soon as the game had ended. She tapped out the number, and when Mrs. Milligan answered on the first ring, Cassie told her where they were, and that Sarah was fine.

Mrs. Milligan said that she and Mr. Milligan had driven to their home, which was only about six blocks from Highland Park. But she said they'd come pick Sarah up in a few minutes.

Cassie said there was no rush, because she and Sarah were headed for Cold Stone.

"We're going to Cold Stone?" Sarah said after Cassie had stuck her phone into her back pocket.

"Ice cream fixes almost everything," Cassie said.

Well, maybe not everything, she thought.

But it couldn't hurt.

Cassie thought there might be another melt when Sarah said she just wanted a bowl of plain vanilla ice cream.

"But this is *Cold Stone*," Cassie said. "Don't you want lots of cool gooey stuff on it?"

"I like vanilla," Sarah said.

Cassie told the boy behind the counter, and he said, "Really?"

"Really," Cassie said, and then ordered Oreo Overload, one of her favorites, for herself.

Cassie paid, having remembered she still had a ten-dollar bill in the back pocket, because she and Jack and the guys had planned to go for ice cream themselves after the game. Then she and Sarah took their bowls and sat at a table by the front window.

Sarah didn't say anything, or even look up, until she'd eaten all of her ice cream, looking as intensely focused on eating ice cream as she did everything else.

When Sarah was finished, Cassie said, "We can get past what happened today."

"No . . . we . . . can't."

Cassie didn't want to argue with her. So all she said was, "It's just the first game."

"I don't care," Sarah said. "Basketball was fun. This isn't."

"It wasn't fun *today*," Cassie said. "But losing is never fun."

Sarah looked down at Cassie's bowl. "You're not eating your ice cream."

"I'd rather talk to you."

"She lied," Sarah said.

"Yeah," Cassie said, "she probably did."

Sarah looked so hard at Cassie that she felt as if she were getting shoved again.

"Not probably. She did."

Cassie nodded, and just pushed her ice cream around with her spoon. "She made a mistake in the game and then felt like she had to try to cover it when the game was over. That's what I think happened."

"But . . . but that's wrong."

"I know it is."

"Nobody stopped her."

"Nobody got the chance," Cassie said. "And even if I believe you, which I do, Sarah, it's still your word against hers."

"And the others will take her word."

"Not all of them."

"A lot of them," Sarah said. She paused and said, "I don't want to do this anymore."

Cassie had placed her phone on the table in front of her, and kept waiting for it to vibrate, and see that Mrs. Milligan was calling. She didn't know how long she had before Sarah's parents got here. But she was going to make the most out of the time she had.

"You're too good to quit," Cassie said. "Not only are you

too good, you're only going to get better."

"If it's not fun, I don't want to play."

"Everybody feels like that from time to time. But things will get better."

"You don't know that."

Cassie felt a smile come all the way up from inside her. She couldn't help it, or stop it.

"Because they can't get any worse!" Cassie said.

About a minute later Cassie's phone did vibrate, and she saw it was a text message from Mrs. Milligan:

Parked in front of bookstore.

"Your mom's here," Cassie said.

Sarah started to get up. Cassie gently placed a hand on her arm. Sarah stared down at it. But sat back down.

"Just show up for our next game against Moran," Cassie said.

"Why, because you think you can make things all better?"

"No," Cassie said. "But my dad will. You can trust him even if you're not ready to trust me."

"How can he fix things?"

"It's a coach thing," Cassie said. "Okay?"

She reached across the table with a closed fist. For a moment she thought Sarah might leave her hanging.

But she didn't.

When Sarah touched Cassie's fist with her own, she did it so lightly, it was like she was afraid she'd break Cassie's hand if she hit it any harder.

"Okay," Sarah said.

Cassie didn't say what was in her head. She just thought it.

Okay, Dad.

You're up.

ELEVEN

The next day Cassie went to watch the next-to-last practice for the Cubs before their season started.

She thought that if she could just sit in the stands and watch her friends play ball, it would take her mind off all the drama with her own team. It did.

Just not for the reasons she thought it would.

As little fun as Sarah Milligan said she was having on the Red Sox, the guys on the Cubs seemed to be having even less. Jack and the guys had told her what the new coach was like. But he was even worse than Cassie had imagined.

And was starting to make Cassie be the one who was afraid of loud noises.

Mr. Anthony somehow managed to keep a smile on his face even when he was chewing somebody out for not taking an extra base, or for throwing to the wrong base, or missing a sign, or even forgetting to take a strike. It was apparently a new rule on the Cubs that every hitter had to take a strike every single time up.

"How many times do I have to tell you that you're not a hitter until you take a strike?" Ken Anthony yelled at Teddy at one point, even though Teddy, obviously having forgotten the rule, had just ripped a vicious foul ball just wide of third base.

"Sorry, Coach," Teddy said.

Cassie was watching Teddy's face, and could see that he wanted to say something more, but she was hoping he wouldn't. And he didn't.

Mr. Anthony was doing the pitching. When Teddy ripped the next strike he saw from him into right field for a clean hit, Mr. Anthony pointed at him and yelled, "*That's* what I'm talking about!"

Cassie had no idea what he was actually talking about. She just had this growing sense that this guy thought he had invented baseball, and that everything on the team somehow revolved around him.

Loudly.

Yeah. He was one of *those* Little League coaches. Having played on her own teams, and having hung around on Jack's and Gus's even before Teddy became a player too, Cassie knew that there weren't as many of them as people thought.

Her dad agreed with her.

"I know coaches like that are the cliché," Chris Bennett had said to her one time.

"Like in the movies," Cassie had said.

"In the movies and even in books," her dad had said. "But the truth is that most of the coaches I've either coached with or against get it. They really do. They understand that it's not about them, that it's always supposed to be about the kids. But too often people watching can't see that—or maybe can't hear that—because of the one or two percent who *don't* get it, who really do think it's all about them, and make such a spectacle of themselves."

Ken Anthony was clearly in the 1 or 2 percent.

He wasn't just having the guys on the Cubs practice like they were playing. He had them practicing like they were playing game seven of the World Series for the real Cubs.

At one point he even decided that Jack, playing shortstop,

had been slow covering second base on a potential double play, even though anybody could see that the ball had been hit too slowly to the Cubs' second baseman, J. B. Scarborough, for them to have had any chance at turning two.

"Game of inches!" Ken Anthony yelled at Jack. "Game of inches. And one of those inches can cost you a run, a game, maybe even a championship. So next time let's get rid of that ball a little sooner."

Cassie was alone in the bleachers, starting to think she was watching more of a baseball detention than practice. But out loud, no one there to hear her, she pretended that she was talking to Coach Ken Anthony.

"What planet are you from?"

In that moment it was almost as if Jack could hear her, or just read her mind, something he did a lot. Because when Cassie looked back at him, he was looking straight at her, grinning, eyebrows raised, as if to say back to her, *Can you believe this guy?*

Cassie shook her head.

No, she could not.

He was absolutely as bad as Teddy had said he was. She really started to think, after less than an hour of watching this, that maybe things on her team weren't nearly as bad as she'd thought they were.

The only time Mr. Anthony managed to calm himself down

was when his son, Sam, took the mound. Cassie knew who he was, because Jack had pointed him out to her when she'd showed up after one of her practices last week.

Sam Anthony was tall, the tallest boy on the team, and looked more like a football player to Cassie than a baseball player, even though big-league baseball players were looking more and more like football players to her all the time. But as big as he was, and as hard as he tried to throw, he didn't look like he had what announcers always called "overpowering stuff."

Cassie frankly didn't think he could throw a ball as hard or as well or as accurately—or even as gracefully—as Jack Callahan did when he was on the mound.

But his father acted as if he were watching a future Hall of Famer when Sam struck out J.B., and then struck out Gus. It wasn't a scrimmage. But there were enough players on the team that the coach could put seven fielders behind Sam, and Teddy behind the plate. Sam's dad, calling balls and strikes, had announced that they were all supposed to pretend that Sam was pitching in a tie game.

Jack came to the plate after Gus.

Cassie knew that Jack wasn't going to help the pitcher out by swinging at the same borderline strikes that J.B. and Gus just had. Jack, even if he did have to take a strike, was going to make Sam Anthony work, waiting for his pitch.

Sam threw a pitch that looked to Cassie to be nearly a foot outside.

"Strike one," his father said. "Caught the corner."

Jack didn't even turn around. Didn't step out of the box. Just stayed in his stance.

The next pitch was farther outside, and Mr. Anthony had no choice but to call it a ball. Same with the next pitch. The count was 2–1.

"How about giving me a better target," Sam called in to Teddy behind the plate, as if missing as badly with the last two pitches was Teddy's fault. Or his mitt's fault.

Teddy had been yelled at enough by Sam's dad today. Cassie could see he wasn't going to take it from his son. He didn't get up, or flip back his mask, and stayed in his crouch. He just put his glove out in front of him, directly behind the plate, the same height as Jack's waist.

"I'm sorry," Teddy called out to Sam. "I didn't realize I was hiding back here."

Cassie heard Mr. Anthony say, "Cool it, Madden. The pitcher always knows best where his target should be."

Now Teddy was the one who didn't turn around. He just nodded and left the mitt exactly where it had been before Sam had chirped on him.

But Sam missed again, enough inside that his dad had no

choice but to give a little shake of his head and say, "Ball three." And Cassie felt herself smiling, because she was a pitcher, and could see what was happening here. This guy was afraid of Jack, even in a glorified batting practice. He was pitching around him, but wanted that to be anybody's fault but his own.

"What are you waiting for, a perfect pitch?"

Now Sam was talking to Jack. But Cassie knew that he could talk to Jack Callahan forever and not get a response out of him.

Jack ignored him. Just took a quick step out of the box with his front foot, adjusted his batting helmet, stepped back in, took his stance, set his hands. Cassie knew that he wasn't waiting for a perfect pitch. Just a strike.

Sam threw one now. Jack put a perfect swing on it, level and lethal. As sweet as the sound of a softball was coming off Cassie's bat, or Sarah's when she really smashed one, this sound, the sound of a hardball, was different.

It had to scare Sam Anthony as soon as he heard it.

Cassie knew this sound, knew the ball was gone as soon as Jack connected. It ended up going high over the left fielder's head, high over the left-field fence. In the distance, Cassie could see the ball finally stop rolling just behind second base on the field on the other side of the outfield fence.

Jack did nothing to show up Sam. He just rounded the bases at a normal speed, not too fast and not too slow. That wasn't the problem. The problem was that when he got to home plate, Teddy gave him a hard low five, a big smile on his face.

As soon as he did, Sam yelled at Teddy, "What, you think this is funny?"

Jack turned around, thinking that Sam might be talking to him again. But then he saw Sam pointing his glove at Teddy.

"What the heck are you talking about?" Teddy said. "We're all on the same team here. I was just congratulating a teammate."

"No, you weren't," Sam said. "You were dogging *me*. And you can't catch me if you're rooting for the batter, even when we're just messing around."

Teddy Madden had clearly heard enough today, from the whole family. He took a step in front of the plate, flipped back his mask now, and said, "I'm not *your* catcher. I'm this team's catcher. Is that some kind of brain buster for you?"

Cassie noticed that Mr. Anthony had come out from behind the plate and had positioned himself between Teddy and Sam. But he didn't talk to his son. He talked to Teddy.

"You need to shut this down right here, son," he said.

Teddy took his mask off. Cassie could see how red his face was. Never a good sign.

"*I* need to shut it?" he said. "I'm not the one who threw that pitch, so we could all see a fastball turn into a *lost* ball."

"Are you back-talking me?" Mr. Anthony said.

His face was suddenly pretty red too.

Watching it all play out, Cassie thought the coach was acting as if Jack had taken *him* deep, not his son.

She didn't realize it, but she'd stood up, thinking: *Please drop this, Teddy. Please don't say one more thing.*

But it was Mr. Anthony who felt he had to add, "Maybe you need to ask yourself whether or not you want to play on my team."

"It's not your team," Teddy said, "any more than I'm your son's catcher."

"I'm gonna say it again," Mr. Anthony said, his voice rising, if such a thing were even possible. "You need to ask yourself whether you want to play on *my* team."

"Maybe I don't," Teddy said.

Then he turned and walked back to his bench and slowly began taking off his equipment, while Mr. Anthony yelled out to the players behind Sam that it was time for everybody to call it a day.

It was when Teddy was in the parking lot with Cassie and Jack and Gus that he said he wasn't just done for the day, he was done for good.

"If it's not fun, what's the point?" he said.

Cassie told him there was a lot of that going around.

TWELVE

Y ou're not quitting," Cassie said to Teddy. "It would make your melt worse than your coach's melt."

"Watch me," Teddy said. "I'm not playing for that guy."

They were on Teddy's back patio, which faced the ball field at Walton Middle School. Mrs. Madden had made iced tea for them, brought out the pitcher and glasses, and even some sliced-up lemons, then gone back into the house. *She knows we have stuff to talk about,* Cassie thought. Mrs. Madden was cool like that.

"You haven't said much," Teddy said to Jack. "What do you think?"

Actually, Jack hadn't said anything. It was one of the things Cassie liked the best about Jack Callahan. He never talked just to talk.

And if there was a captain of their crew, it was Jack. Even Cassie knew it. He was the same kind of natural leader with them that he was on every sports team on which he'd ever played.

Cassie knew why Teddy was asking. Not only did he want to know what Jack thought, he wanted Jack's approval, especially when it came to sports. They all knew they wouldn't even be here, having this conversation, if Jack hadn't stood up for Teddy in seventh grade when he was being bullied by some of the other kids at school for being overweight and out of shape, back when some of those kids had nicknamed him Teddy Bear. But Jack had helped him get *into* shape. Then Teddy and everybody else had found out that there was an athlete inside him, a good one. And a tough one.

But now it was as if he were being bullied all over again, by Coach Anthony.

"I think Cassie's right," Jack said. "You can't quit. And you're not going to quit."

"You're there every day!" Teddy said. "You and Gus know what a jerk he is."

"Not arguing that with you," Jack said. "I bet even his own son knows what a jerk he is."

"I'm not getting picked on all summer," Teddy said. "If I want to do that, I can just hang with Cassie more."

She reached over before he could move his arm, and pinched him.

"We're trying to help you, and you take a shot?" she said. "Seriously?"

"That was seriously funny," Teddy said.

"Moderately," she said.

Teddy nodded. "I can live with that."

Okay, she thought. *There's hope.* He was still trying to use humor, as hurt and angry as he clearly was. Maybe he was still set on quitting. But Cassie remembered a line her mother liked to use, one she said she'd read in a book about the movies written by William Goldman, who'd written one of Cassie's all-time favorite books, *The Princess Bride.*

Maybe Teddy wasn't set-set.

"If you quit," Jack said, keeping his voice even, eyes on Teddy, "then that guy wins."

Before Teddy could respond, Jack added, "And what I've

found out being your teammate is that you hate to lose as much as any of us."

"I managed to survive losing the championship game in football," Teddy said.

He had survived. It had been his first season of organized football, and once he'd made the team, he was supposed to be their tight end. But then Jack had gotten hurt, and it had turned out Teddy had the best arm of anybody else on the team, and he'd turned out to be a terrific quarterback, all the way to the championship game, when the other team just ended up with the ball last.

Cassie said, "That was different and you know it."

"How was it different?"

"Because you *didn't* quit that day."

"You're right about that," Teddy said. "I didn't quit. We just ran out of time."

"It was like the other team got the last word," Gus said.

Jack said to Teddy, "You can't let Coach Anthony, or Sam, get the last word on you."

"That's not what this is about."

"Yeah," Cassie said, "it is. And it's about you being better than them."

Teddy took a long drink of iced tea, put his glass down, put his head back, closed his eyes, and shook his head. No jokes from him now. Cassie could just tell from his tone of voice. He was speaking from the heart.

"He makes me not want to go to practice," he said. "It's not just that he yells at me. He's yelling all the time, like he's always got the volume turned all the way up. Sometimes, swear, the last thing I hear when I close my eyes at night is the sound of his stupid voice."

"Same," Gus said.

"I think it might happen to me tonight too," Cassie said. She tried to imitate Coach Anthony, making her voice deeper. And louder. *"Game of inches!"* Then she was back in her own voice, saying, "I almost laughed when he said that, but I was afraid if I did, he'd call me out of the bleachers and make me run some laps."

"Maybe on his days off from us, he can come bark at your team," Gus said.

"And you know what another crazy part of this is?" Cassie said. "His son's not even that good!"

"Tell me about it," Teddy said.

They sat in silence then. They could do that sometimes when they were together, even Teddy, who out of all of them was the one who liked to talk the most. Cassie didn't want to push him right now, just because he'd calmed down so much in the past few minutes.

Finally Teddy said, "You know it's not just baseball, right? You wait the whole school year, even when you're having fun playing other sports, waiting for summer. And I don't want this guy to ruin mine."

Cassie turned to him, and started to speak, but Teddy put up a hand. "Let me finish," he said. "I think a lot about stuff like that. I think about how good we have it, just having each other. But guess what? Before long we're going to be in high school. I mean, what the heck? That means we've got five more summers, counting this one, before we're in *college*. We've got to make all of them count, is all I'm saying."

"Teddy's right," Gus said. "I think about stuff like that too. I just don't talk about it as much." He grinned. "But then, I don't talk about anything as much as Teddy does."

"Hey," Teddy said. "You're one of my wingmen, remember?"

"But I can't lie, Cass," Gus said. "I feel the same way about Coach as Teddy does."

"Then we gotta find a way to power through," Jack said. "We've all done that with teammates we didn't like."

"They were teammates," Gus said, "not the boss of us."

"You're the boss of you when it comes to baseball," Jack said. "Same with Teddy. Same with all of us. Nobody can make us *not* love baseball."

"I've been trying to explain the same thing to Sarah," Cassie said. "I can see how much she wants to be a good softball player, how much she wants to be a part of a team, and belong. I told her that she can't let some of the girls on our team make her forget that."

"You're not playing for Coach," Jack said to Teddy. "You're playing for you, and for us. Not him."

"But what about Sam?" Teddy said. "He's no better than his father. And I'm supposed to catch him and act like I want him to do well?"

"Yup," Cassie said. "Because it's not about him, either. It's about the team."

Teddy pointed at her first, then Jack, then back at Cassie. "You two know how much you sound alike, right?"

Cassie smiled. "Yes," she said. "And I just hope Jack appreciates how lucky he is to sound like me."

"So, *so* much," Jack said.

Jack looked at Teddy again. As always, when Jack had as much to say as he did today, it wasn't just Teddy paying attention to him. They all did.

"You've come too far in sports to quit now," Jack said to Teddy. "Baseball's gotten too important to you, and you're too important to our team to walk away."

"Basically," Cassie said, "it's not about asking if you want to play for him. It's asking yourself why you want to play in the first place."

Teddy was quiet again. Cassie knew this look too. It was as if he were having a conversation with himself that only he could hear. Finally he nodded, got up, opened the sliding door to his kitchen. When he came back a couple of minutes later, he was holding a Wiffle ball and bat.

"I'm not making any promises about sticking it out with this meathead," he said. "But I will for now."

"Okay, then," Gus said.

"Okay," Jack said.

"I hate it when you guys are right," Teddy said.

"We know," Cassie said. Then she told the boys to pick sides for home-run derby, she didn't care what team she was on.

But she was batting first.

THIRTEEN

Cassie's dad scheduled an extra practice on Monday night that he told Cassie wasn't really going to be a practice at all. It was going to be a team meeting instead, he just wasn't telling the rest of the girls beforehand.

"We need to get this thing with Kathleen and Sarah squared away," he said, "so we can go forward as a team."

"Kathleen's the one who turned it into a thing," Cassie said when they were in the car and on their way to Highland Park.

"I know."

"And you know I believe Sarah," Cassie said.

"You have made that abundantly clear, kiddo."

"What about you?"

"Between you and me?" he said. "So do I."

"But that means Kathleen is lying."

"Know that, too."

"I just don't think Sarah has it in her to lie," Cassie said. "I really don't."

"My job is finding a way to keep the peace without calling Kathleen out on her lie," her dad said.

"Good luck with that," Cassie said.

"Kathleen's not a bad kid."

"She's still being an idiot."

"She's being a kid," her dad said.

"You make it sound like the same thing?" Cassie asked.

"Only sometimes," he said. "And not just with kids, by the way."

She thought of the way Coach Anthony acted. "I hear you," Cassie said to her dad.

"Now let's hope the rest of the team does too," her dad said.

They rode the rest of the way to the field with the inside of the car completely quiet.

When the whole team was there, Cassie's dad told them to

leave their gloves and bat bags at the bench, that they might do some soft-tossing later and a few fielding drills, but he'd really gathered them here to talk.

Chris Bennett walked the entire team out to left-center field, where all the action had taken place at the end of Saturday's game. The players on the Red Sox arranged themselves in a circle around him.

"So," he said, "we all know what happened in our first game, and I'm pretty sure that nobody is happy about the way things ended."

Cassie looked around at her teammates. Her dad had their full attention. Sometimes Cassie saw a little bit of her dad in Jack, the way there was just something about his manner, the way he naturally presented himself, that made people pay attention to him when he was talking. Cassie knew because she felt it all the time, whether they were in the car on their way to practice, or at the dinner table, or when she and her dad were watching a ball game together.

"It's not my intent," he continued, "to go over the whole thing again, moment by moment. Because it's a funny thing when things are happening in a moment. People can see them completely differently. When I was in college, I took this course on the movies, and one of the movies we studied was called *Rashomon*. It was actually Japanese. But the point of it was about this crime that was committed in the woods, and how four different people saw it four different ways."

Cassie glanced across at Kathleen. She was glaring at Cassie's dad, as if somehow she knew where this was going and she already didn't like it.

"That's what might have happened with Kathleen and Sarah," he said. "And maybe the truth is just somewhere in between them, the way that softball was out here."

Sarah was sitting next to Cassie. She hadn't said a word to anybody, had barely looked at anybody, since she'd arrived at the field. For now, Cassie was just happy that Sarah had kept her part of their deal. She was here, even if she didn't much look as if she wanted to be.

"But *whatever* happened," Chris Bennett said, "we need to find a way to put it behind us before we can move forward as a group, and as a team."

He slowly made a full circle, as a way of looking at every face.

"And I honestly believe that the only way for us to be able to do it is to clear the air right now," he said. He stopped his turn and looked at Kathleen. "Kath," he said, "is there anything you'd like to say to Sarah?"

There was no hesitation from her. None. And no change of expression.

"No."

"Well," Cassie's dad said, "there's something that I'd like you to say to her."

Kathleen crossed her arms in front of her.

"What?" she said.

"I'd like you to apologize to Sarah for calling her a liar," Chris Bennett said.

"Sorry, Mr. Bennett," Kathleen said. "But I'm not doing that."

Cassie turned slightly so she could see Sarah's face. She wasn't looking at Kathleen. She was looking at Cassie's dad and had crossed her arms too. But with her it was almost as if she were hugging herself. She looked as if she were afraid in that moment that she might fly apart.

Kathleen said, "So you're taking *her* side?"

She pointed at Sarah. And before Cassie's dad could answer, Kathleen then pointed at Cassie and said, "And that must mean you are too, right?"

"This isn't about Cassie," Chris Bennett said. "This is between you and Sarah."

"Oh, we all know this *is* about Cassie, too. Her and her new friend. Maybe I should push you to the ground, Cassie, to get in better with you."

Keeping her voice calm, Cassie said, "Kathleen, when have you ever *not* been in good with me?"

"Well, if we're so tight," Kathleen said, "then who do *you* believe, me or her?"

There it was, right in the middle of the circle. And Cassie knew that whatever answer she was going to give wasn't just about Kathleen and Sarah Milligan and a ball that had fallen between them. In this moment she was being asked a question about character. Her parents, both of them, had always told her that character was character even if you were alone in a room. It was about making the right choice, even when the right choice was the hardest.

"Okay," Cassie said. "Even though I don't think it's the worst thing that's ever happened in the world, I believe you messed up on that play and felt so badly afterward that you blamed it on Sarah."

Kathleen sprang to her feet. "So you're saying *I'm* the liar? Is that what you're saying?"

"I just don't think you told the truth," Cassie said.

"It's the same thing!" Kathleen said.

"Kathleen," Cassie's dad said, "what happened on that play happens all the time in baseball. The real truth is that sometimes it's just miscommunication. The only two people who really know what happened out there are you and Sarah. But what I know is that it's my job as the coach of this team to not let one blown play blow up our season after just one game. Over a ball that maybe neither one of you could have caught anyway."

Kathleen turned now to look at Greta, and Allie, and all the girls who were sitting closest to her. "Do you guys believe them too?" she said.

Greta and Allie gave quick shakes of their heads.

Kathleen turned back to Cassie's dad and said, "Since I'm such a horrible person, do you even want me on this team?"

"I never said you were a horrible person, Kath," Cassie's dad said. "Come on."

"Well, *do* you?"

"You're a very good player, and I've always enjoyed coaching you. And you know what everybody out here knows, that we've got a chance to be great this season, and one loss doesn't change that. I very much want you to be a part of all that. And I can't force you to apologize. But I still think it would be better for everybody if you did."

Kathleen was talking again to Greta and Allie and the girls next to them. "Do you believe this?" she said.

When she turned back to the rest of the group, she pointed at Sarah again and said, "She's the one who should be apologizing. To *me*."

Sarah spoke for the first time, her voice barely more than a whisper. "No," she said, almost as if talking to herself. "No, no, no."

Kathleen said, "I'm not listening to this anymore."

To Cassie's dad she said, "Do I have to stay?"

"No," he said, his voice sounding sad as he did. "No, you don't."

"Do any of us have to stay if we don't want to?" Kathleen said.

"You don't," Chris Bennett said. "And it looks as if we're done here, anyway."

"Then I'm leaving," Kathleen said. She looked around and said, "Anybody else?"

Greta stood up. Allie did. So did most of the other players on the team, surprising Cassie. Lizzie stayed put. So did Brooke. Cassie and Sarah. That was it. The rest of the Red Sox players followed Kathleen back toward the infield.

Cassie's dad had come here tonight hoping he could bring the team together. Now the opposite had happened. And now Cassie's dad was the one who seemed to be talking to himself.

"Well," he said, "that went well."

"This is all my fault," Sarah said. "Allmyfaultallmyfaultall-myfault."

By now Cassie knew that Sarah often repeated herself when she was under pressure.

In almost the exact same moment, both Cassie and her dad said, "No, it's not."

But Cassie was starting to wonder if that one stupid ball between two of their outfielders was ever going to stop rolling.

FOURTEEN

All of the players who had walked off with Kathleen the night before showed up for the Red Sox game against the Moran Mariners, another home game for them before they'd play their next two games on the road.

Anybody watching Cassie and her teammates warm up on this night might not have noticed anything different about them, during batting practice, during infield practice, or when Allie's dad was hitting fly balls to the outfielders.

But Cassie did.

The players who had followed Kathleen weren't speaking to Cassie, and were doing everything possible to ignore her. They were even keeping eye contact to a minimum. The only time Kathleen and Greta and Allie and the rest of them *did* make eye contact, it was to see if Cassie was walking toward them, so that they could casually walk in a different direction.

Lizzie was still talking to her. She lived three doors down and had been Cassie's friend since they were in preschool together. So was Brooke Connors, who had played softball and soccer and basketball with Cassie the longest, until Cassie had played on the boys' team last winter. But Kathleen and Greta and Allie had also played on Cassie's teams for a long time. They had all done a lot of winning together. Now, at least in Cassie's view, they were acting like losers.

"What's up with this?" Cassie said to Lizzie. "They're acting like I'm going to play for Moran tonight."

They were standing behind the Red Sox bench. Kathleen and Greta and Allie, and a new girl on the team this year, Maria Castellanos, had gone down the right-field line to play catch. But Cassie could see them occasionally staring in at her.

Lizzie said, "There was a group chat last night."

"Were you on it?" Cassie said.

"Everybody on our team was on it," Lizzie said.

"Except me."

"You and Sarah."

"She's never been on our group chats," Cassie said. She actually felt a smile coming up out of her. "And you know that I do everything possible to stay *off* them."

"This wasn't our old group chat," Lizzie said. "This was a new one they started last night."

"And the point of it was giving me the silent treatment?"

Lizzie said, "Pretty much."

"Anything else?" Cassie said.

"Yeah," Lizzie said. "They said that players on our team had to decide whether they were with them, or with you."

FIFTEEN

What was happening went against everything that Cassie thought about teams and what they were supposed to be about.

Because there were two teams today:

Hers and Kathleen's.

Like they'd chosen sides for a pickup game.

Except that Cassie had Sarah and Lizzie and Brooke, and Kathleen had everybody else.

But even with all that, even though their team had now splintered like an old wooden baseball bat, they were all supposed to have the same common goal, which meant trying to win the game, trying not to start the season 0–2, trying to keep their eye on the same prize, making it to Fenway Park, getting to play what would feel to them like a softball World Series, getting to play some games on TV. It suddenly seemed to Cassie like a pretty long time ago that they were worried about being the best team in their league, maybe even going undefeated the way they had last summer.

Cassie had always believed that one of the big keys in sports was just getting out of your own way. And even if some of her teammates couldn't get out of their own way tonight, she wasn't going to let them get in hers. If they wanted to obsess about stuff that had nothing to do with winning the game, let them. She wasn't wired that way. She was here to do what she always had: Play her own game and try to win her team's. That was it and that was all.

She was here to play, not talk.

If Kathleen and Greta and Allie and the rest of them didn't want to talk to her, their choice. She wasn't going to push it, or push them. She'd read somewhere once about an old Boston Celtics coach who talked about how different basketball and baseball were, starting with the fact that there were only five players on the court for your team in basketball.

"In baseball," the coach said, "it doesn't matter whether the left fielder knows the catcher's name."

Cassie didn't agree with him. She loved being on teams, loved the relationships, *hated* what was happening with the Red Sox. But she understood what the guy was talking about. Once the game started, she just hoped that everybody would figure it out. If everything was less social than it used to be, well, they were all just going to have to deal.

Do your job, she told herself.

She told Sarah the same thing before they took the field. Brooke was pitching tonight, so Cassie was back at shortstop. Maria was catching. Other than that, their team looked pretty much the same, even though it wasn't.

"I always try to do my job," Sarah said.

"I know," Cassie said.

"I don't think of it as a job," Sarah said.

It occurred to Cassie again how literally Sarah could take the simplest comments.

"Well, I'm giving you one job tonight," Cassie said. "If there is a ball between you and one of the other outfielders, call for it so loudly, they can hear you in Moran."

"Okay," Sarah said.

MIKE LUPICA

They took the field then, Cassie leading them out the way she always did. When she took her position between second and third, Kathleen ran right past her, not looking at Cassie, not slowing down.

Cassie said to herself, "Go, team."

Cassie had the feeling that before they went a lot deeper into the season, Sarah was going to become one of their starting pitchers, just having seen her pitch from the mound a few times in practice. And if she could bring it in a game the way she did in practice, it would just make the Red Sox stronger, because Brooke wasn't just the best catcher they had, she was the best catcher in their league.

Brooke liked being a catcher more, but she was a pretty good softball pitcher, too, and through the early innings she was pitching beautifully, shutting out the Mariners through the third. Cassie's dad had tweaked their batting order just a little tonight, putting Lizzie at leadoff, following her with Kathleen, then Cassie and Sarah and Greta and Brooke after that. And it worked out right away, bottom of the first. Lizzie singled, Kathleen walked, Cassie doubled home both of them, Sarah singled home Cassie. It was Sarah's first hit of the season. When she got to first base, it was almost as if she didn't know what to do with herself, or how to act, until Lizzie's dad, who was helping out by coaching first tonight, reached over and gave her a low five. From the bench Cassie could only see Sarah's face in profile. But she thought Sarah was smiling.

Just like that it was 3–0. After the way they'd struggled offensively against Hollis Hills, they'd come out swinging tonight. In the third Brooke helped herself by hitting her first home run of the season and the team's first home run.

For these few innings, this season looked an awful lot like last season. It just didn't sound like last season, especially in the bench area. Everything was just much quieter than it used to be. When Brooke got back to the bench after her home run, only Cassie and Sarah and Lizzie were up to greet her. Before they went back out onto the field for the top of the fourth, Cassie's dad pulled her aside and said, "Okay, what's going on here?"

As softly as she could, Cassie said, "Some of my friends have decided to freeze me out. And freeze out anybody who's still talking to me."

"C'mon," he said, "we can't have that and be a real team."

"*Dad,*" Cassie said. "Leave it alone. Or it will become a bigger thing than it already is. And they'll think I went running to you because they're being mean to me."

"But this is ridiculous."

MIKE LUPICA

"I know," she said. "Let me handle it."

It made him grin. "Gee," he said, "never heard that one before."

The Red Sox kept their lead into the fifth, but barely. Brooke walked the first two batters and then gave up back-to-back screaming doubles, and the 4–0 game was 4–3, in what felt like a blink. The Mariners finally ended up with the bases loaded, but with two outs Cassie dove to her left for a ball hit hard up the middle by the Mariners' first baseman, somehow gloved the ball cleanly and flipped it to Allie for the final out of the inning.

Usually a play like that, one that saved two runs at least, would have gotten her a high five from Allie. Not today. All Allie did after the infield umpire signaled that the runner at second was out was toss the ump the ball and run off the field. But Allie did get a high five from Greta, waiting for her near first base.

Yeah, Cassie thought, *because Allie didn't drop a perfect toss that a five-year-old could have caught.*

Whatever. They were still ahead by a run. That was the important thing. And they stayed ahead by a run through the bottom of the sixth until Cassie tripled home Lizzie, giving them a two-run cushion going into the last inning. Brooke was through for the night by then. She went back behind the plate, Maria went to second, and Allie came in to pitch the top of the seventh. Usually, after she finished her warm-up pitches and the infielders had thrown the ball around, Cassie would bring the ball into the mound and stuff it into Allie's glove, maybe ask if she had all the runs she needed. She started to do that tonight, then stopped about ten feet from the mound and just tossed Allie the ball underhand, the way she had to end the fifth.

As Cassie ran back to short, she called over to Lizzie and said, "We got this."

And Lizzie said, "Which ones of us?"

Cassie got into her ready position, hoping what she always did: that somebody would hit a ball to her. Not all of her teammates felt the same way in close games. They'd told her so, at least when they were still talking to her, admitted they *never* wanted the ball hit to them in a big spot. But Cassie did.

But she didn't get her chance to pitch the seventh. The first Moran batter, Kelly Wasserman, who'd been the Mariners' starting pitcher, hit what looked like a routine ground ball to Greta's right at first base. Not routine. Greta booted it like the soccer player she was.

Cassie thought: *Well, maybe we* don't *have this after all.*

Allie walked the next batter.

MIKE LUPICA

First and second, nobody out.

The Mariners were still down two but had a great big inning shaping up, because Allie looked as shaky now as she had in their first game. Cassie took one step toward the mound, and then stopped herself. Usually she'd call time and run over there and give Allie a pep talk. But she wasn't doing that today, because she didn't know what would happen when she got to the mound, whether she'd be adding more drama and more pressure to a situation that seemed to have enough already.

Allie managed to strike out the Mariners' catcher, the girl getting overanxious and swinging at a 3–2 pitch up in her eyes. But the next batter ripped a single to left. Kathleen had no chance for a play at the plate but threw home anyway, the ball sailing over Lizzie's head when Lizzie set herself up to be the cutoff. Brooke had to run into foul territory to catch the ball, and when she did, both runners advanced.

Second and third now, one-run game, still just one out. Tying run at third, go-ahead run at second.

"Just get an out," Cassie yelled out from short now, the words just coming out of her. Or the ballplayer coming out of her. Allie was still her teammate, even if she and a lot of her teammates were acting like idiots.

Allie didn't act as if she'd heard. Cassie didn't care whether she had or not.

She thought: *Get an out.*

And keep the runner at third.

Allie got an out. The Mariners' shortstop swung at a pitch that was too far inside, getting jammed, and badly. She made contact with the ball, hit a soft, looping liner over Allie's head. Allie had no chance at the ball by the time she got herself turned around. But Cassie read the ball all the way. It still wasn't an easy play, because she had to come a fair distance from short. She ended up going to her knees to make a sliding catch, her glove pocket-up, what her dad called a basket catch.

Allie had kept the ball in the infield. Kept the runner at third. Two outs now. And all of a sudden this felt like more than just the second game of the season. Cassie knew that the Red Sox getting their first win of the season wasn't going to change anything except their record, at least not tonight. Wasn't going to make things any louder around their team. But maybe, she thought, just maybe, if they *could* get out of this with a win, it could be the start of something. Maybe better days.

The Mariners' best hitter, Karen Dale, their third baseman, was at the plate. Cassie had been playing against her since they'd both started playing softball. Karen could hit, could field her position, didn't show off or chirp, and had always played the game right. It had always been big fun competing against her, especially when Cassie was pitching.

Now Cassie just wanted Karen to hit her the ball.

Only, she didn't.

What she did was hit the first ball she saw from Allie high and deep to center field. You didn't even have to track the flight of the ball. You could just *hear* the sound it made coming off Karen's bat.

All Cassie could do was turn and watch.

This one wasn't in the gap between Sarah and Kathleen. No, this one was directly over Sarah's head.

Cassie thought it was gone.

Sarah Milligan clearly didn't.

Cassie wasn't sure how Sarah, having been on the team this short a time, knew the things she knew about being a softball player. Maybe you had to be born with some of them. Or all of them. Maybe it was the same for everybody, even if people thought you were different.

In this moment Sarah knew enough to run to the spot where she thought the ball was headed, run with her head down, looking up one time to see where the fence was, knowing that she was about to run out of space. Or time.

At the very last second, maybe ten feet from the sign on the fence that said WALTON MOBIL STATION, she turned back, looked up, and reached up with her glove.

The ball landed in it. And stayed in it, even as Sarah was reaching out with her free hand to stop herself from running into the fence. Sarah didn't hit the fence hard but still lost her balance enough to end up sitting at the base of the fence.

Kathleen didn't run over to help her up, or congratulate her. Neither did Ellie Evans, their right fielder in the late innings tonight. Sarah picked herself up, then held her glove aloft to show the umpire who'd come running out from the infield that the ball was still in it.

The woman put her own hand in the air, fist closed, pumping it as she made the *out* sign.

Ball game.

By now Cassie had gone flying past the ump, running in Sarah's direction, Lizzie behind her. She reminded herself not to startle Sarah Milligan this time, or even try to high five her.

She just stopped a few feet away, smiling, and said, "Well, that catch didn't stink."

Sarah didn't seem to know how to respond. She just reached out and handed Cassie the ball, as if she were done with it.

When she and Lizzie and Cassie turned around, they saw

all the members of their team who had been on the field for the last play of the game just staring at them, as if they were all frozen in place.

This time it was Sarah Milligan who allowed herself a small smile as she said to Cassie and Lizzie, "Now you guys know how I feel."

SIXTEEN

Cassie invited Sarah over for lunch the next day, and Sarah accepted.

Cassie wasn't kidding herself. She didn't feel as if she and Sarah were getting a lot closer, or becoming friends, at least the way Cassie defined friendship. She wasn't sure what they were, apart from being teammates. Maybe more like allies. But for now that seemed to be enough for both of them. Maybe it was all Sarah could handle. Another thing Cassie had read about kids with Asperger's was how hard it was to earn their trust, as they did their best to keep the world at arm's length.

Sarah rode her bike over. When she got to Cassie's house, she made a big point of telling Cassie the exact route she'd taken, street by street. Then she explained how she'd be going home, giving Cassie the streets in reverse.

"I'm not sure I could remember that without GPS," Cassie said.

"I know what GPS is," Sarah said. "Do people use it when they ride bikes?"

"I was joking."

"Oh. Right."

They were up in Cassie's room after lunch, Cassie on her bed, Sarah in the same chair she'd been in the night she'd come to the house with her parents. But today Cassie noticed her taking in the whole room. The first night here, she'd paid no attention to the big globe in the corner, but today she got up and walked over to it, almost as if drawn to it, and slowly turned it, moving a finger across it, as if she were trying to imagine the route she'd take from Cassie's house to Europe, or Asia.

"I know most of the world's capitals. Do you?" Sarah said suddenly, her voice rising in excitement.

Cassie had noticed by now that Sarah either couldn't or wouldn't modulate her voice. The girl who hated loud noises often got loud herself, sometimes right before her voice would almost drop to a whisper.

She began to recite some of the capitals now, Brussels and Paris and Helsinki and Budapest, London and Warsaw and Lisbon, almost as if Cassie wasn't even in the room with her.

"That is impressive, Sarah, not gonna lie."

Sarah ignored her and kept going. "Amsterdam," she said. "Dublin. Athens. Reykjavik. Oslo."

She paused, looking right at Cassie now, and said, "Do you know what Riga is the capital of?"

"Nope."

Sarah nodded. "Latvia," she said.

"The only thing I know about Latvia," Cassie said, "is that one of the Knicks comes from there."

"I know."

"You do?

"He comes from Liepaja," Sarah said, and nodded. "I had to look that up. I know a lot of different things. If I don't know them, I look them up. I like to look things up and then memorize them. If I close my eyes, I can see all the streets I took here and the ones I'm going to take back. It's very important. Very, very important."

This was one of those times, Cassie thought, when Sarah looked more comfortable talking to herself, instead of going back and forth with somebody else.

Sarah carefully turned the globe now, as if she were afraid that spinning it too hard might break it.

"Do you think the other girls are being stupid?" she said. "I do. I think they're being stupid."

"More stubborn than stupid, maybe."

"I think they're being stupid and mean," Sarah said, not acting as if she'd even heard Cassie. "My mom tells me all the time that sometimes other kids don't mean to be stupid or mean, they just don't know any better. But they barely know me. They know you. So why are they treating us the same?"

"If you want to know the truth," Cassie said, "sometimes I think they don't know me at all. But it still makes them mad when I don't go along with them."

"I hate when people get mad." She gave the globe another small turn. If you looked at her, it was almost as if she were talking to it instead of Cassie.

She stopped talking now and walked back over and sat down in her chair, as if she had run out of things to say. She folded her hands in her lap and finally said that it was probably time for her to go. Cassie checked her phone, saw what time it was, and remembered that the Cubs were practicing earlier than usual that afternoon, four o'clock at Highland Park, before their first game.

"You mind if I ride with you?" Cassie said. "I know I won't get lost."

"I never get lost," Sarah said, her face serious. "I know the way." And then once again she recited the streets that would take her past Highland Park and home. She looked at Cassie now and said, "Why do you want to ride with me?"

"My friends Jack and Teddy and Gus are practicing in the park, and I thought I'd go watch."

"Can I watch too?"

"Sounds like a plan," Cassie said.

Just one she hadn't thought through as well as she might have.

They actually heard Coach Anthony before they parked their bikes near the bleachers on the home side of Highland Park.

"Morales!" was the first thing they heard. "How many times do I have to tell you where the runner has to be before you decide to cut the ball off?"

So, Cassie thought, it was Gus's turn to be in the barrel, as her dad liked to say. If Sarah had heard, she didn't let on. But Cassie sure had. She assumed that even moms and little kids at the playground in the distance could hear.

"Great," Cassie said.

"What's great?"

"Nothing."

When they took their seats halfway up the bleachers, Cassie saw that the Cubs were doing a drill that had runners on the bases, and the outfielders trying to throw them out if they could.

Gus was at first. Jack was at short. Mr. Anthony had a bat in his hands at home plate. Teddy was behind him. Sam Anthony, Cassie saw, was one of the base runners, at second. Brett Hawkins, who was playing both the infield and outfield this season, was on first. Gregg Leonard was in center today. Scott Sutter, who'd been the catcher last season before he'd gotten hurt and opened up the position for Teddy, was in left. Max Conte was in right.

"Two outs, runners going as soon as I hit this ball," Mr. Anthony called out to the guys on defense.

"It will be hard to throw out the man at second on a single if the runners are running," Sarah said.

"Probably."

"Do you think I could do it?"

Cassie grinned. "Definitely."

"You have to charge the ball," Sarah said. "You have to go fast but not rush when you pick the ball up. Field it cleanly. Then come up throwing." She nodded. "Then concentrate on squaring yourself up and not rushing the throw, because that's when you make a wild throw."

"Did you get that from my dad?" Cassie said.

"*My* dad," Sarah said. "Over and over and over and over again. That's how I get things down. You have to concentrate on the fundamentals. If you concentrate on the fundamentals, they'll come naturally in a game. Fundamentals and repetition, those are the keys."

She sounded the way she had when she was reciting the capitals of Europe. Not just secure in this repetition, Cassie thought, but happy.

Mr. Anthony hit a line drive over second base to Gregg Leonard, who did exactly what Sarah had said he should do: he charged the ball, gloved it cleanly, squared himself, and came up throwing. As he did, Cassie checked to see where Sam Anthony was and was surprised to see that he couldn't have taken off when his dad had hit the ball, because he had just come around third base. If he hadn't been running hard enough before, he was now.

His father had gotten out of the way. Teddy wasn't blocking the plate yet. In youth baseball they used the same new rules about blocking the plate that they did in the big leagues. Cassie knew that Major League Baseball had changed the rules after Buster Posey of the Giants had gotten crushed on a play at the plate and been lost to his team for the season.

So Teddy held his position, holding his glove out, waiting

for Gregg's throw. Gus was the cutoff man. He was in perfect position, and Gregg's throw went directly over him, and into Teddy's glove on one bounce.

"Wow," Cassie heard Sarah say. "Wow, wow, wow."

When Teddy had the ball, he quickly moved to his left, Cassie once again admiring how good his footwork was, how far he'd come as a catcher in just a year. So now he was set up between Sam Anthony and the plate, and you could see that the play wasn't even going to be close when Sam went into his slide—because you had to slide. Nobody was allowed to run over the catcher.

Sam didn't try to run Teddy over.

But it wasn't exactly a straight slide, either, because he was way too close to Teddy when he went into it, and went into Teddy with his feet way too high as Teddy put the tag on him.

Sam's lead leg caught Teddy in the middle of his chest protector, and sent him over onto his back, in a huge explosion of dirt at home plate.

And now Cassie said, "Wow, wow, wow."

Teddy was up so fast, it was as if he had springs in his legs. The ball was still in his mitt, but with his free hand he pulled off his mask and tossed it behind him.

"What kind of punk move was *that*?" Teddy shouted, pointing his mitt at Sam.

By now Sam was on his feet too.

"Just trying to knock the ball loose, like I was taught," Sam shouted back at him.

Cassie had seen Teddy angry before. Never this angry.

"What class was that taught in," Teddy said, his voice still hot, "the one about dirty play?"

"You calling me a dirty player?"

Teddy took another step closer to Sam now. Sam took a step back. Cassie wondered if Sam even knew he'd done it.

"If you wanted to come in high, why didn't you just try to run me over?" Teddy said.

"Think I couldn't?"

"No," Teddy said.

He took another step forward. Sam took another step back.

"No," Teddy said. "I don't."

Cassie wondered when Sam's dad was going to step in and break them up. In the practices she'd watched so far, this was the longest he'd ever gone without raising his own voice.

Jack appeared now, putting himself between Teddy and Sam. Jerry York had come down from third base to get his arms around Sam from behind.

"You want to go?" Sam yelled, even though Cassie had a feeling, the way he'd thrown himself into reverse, that he didn't.

"So much," Teddy said.

"All right," Coach Anthony finally yelled over both of them, "that's enough, from both of you!"

They all heard what came next.

"Stop it! Stop it, all of you! Everybody stop being mean!"

Sarah.

"Stop yelling!"

Louder than all of them.

An amazing thing happened then.

They did.

SEVENTEEN

Sarah didn't wait to see what was going to happen now that the yelling had stopped. She just went down the bleachers two at a time without saying good-bye to Cassie and hopped onto her bike and rode away.

Cassie stayed.

The whole Cubs team was gathered around the home plate area. She couldn't hear what anybody was saying now, just could see that Mr. Anthony was doing most of the talking.

When he finished, she waited to see if Teddy and Sam were going to shake hands, make some kind of peace, at least for now. If they did, she didn't see it happen.

She quietly moved down out of the bleachers and up to the fence, in time to hear Mr. Anthony say, "See you tomorrow night. Batting practice at five sharp."

Cassie watched Mr. Anthony and Sam leave together and thought, *Their team is just divided in a different way right now. It wasn't just one new player. It was this new coach.* But when he and his son were gone, the rest of the Cubs were still there, seemingly in no hurry to leave.

Then an odd thing happened. Or maybe a cool thing. Jack went and grabbed a bat and gestured for the other guys to take their positions. Brett went out to short to take Jack's place. And for the next fifteen minutes, Jack hit ground balls to the infielders and fly balls to the outfielders. Suddenly they were all chirping at each other and laughing sometimes, as if they all needed to remember why they were here, why they were ballplayers, maybe even why they loved baseball, before they went home.

When they were done, Cassie came through the fence and sat next to Teddy while he took off his equipment. Jack and Gus sat in the grass in front of them.

"So," she said, "how's the season going so far for all of us?"

"Ours hasn't even started yet," Teddy said.

Cassie said, "What did Mr. Anthony say about that play?"

"Totally wimped out, for a guy who thinks he's so tough," Teddy said. "Said he didn't have the best angle on the play, but it seemed like it just might have been overaggressive baserunning to him."

"Well, yeah," Gus said, "only if you're looking to start a bench-clearing brawl."

"Looked to me," Cassie said, "as if he was trying to make up for the fact that he dogged it when the ball was hit."

"Emphasis on 'dog,'" Teddy said.

"Did you say anything to Coach?" Cassie said.

"I don't call him that," Teddy said. "Not *gonna* call him that. I just think of him as that jerk's dad. But, no, I didn't say anything. No point. He was never going to go against Sam."

"How did you guys end it?" Cassie said.

"He told us that not everybody on the team had to like each other to win with each other," Teddy said. "Another one of his dopey sayings."

"Hey," she said, "look on the bright side."

"There's a bright side?" Gus said.

"At least you guys don't have almost the whole team mad at you like I do."

"Well, I feel better already," Teddy said.

"Looks like we've all got stuff to work through, basically," she said.

"You *think?*" Teddy said.

"Cass is right," Jack said. "We're all gonna have to figure it out."

"The best part of the whole thing was when Sarah did what we all want to do with Mr. Anthony," Teddy said, "and told him to shut up."

Gus said, "Can she come to all our practices? Please?"

"I didn't get the chance to tell her that, see, we aren't the only one with a messed-up team," Cassie replied.

It was still early enough, and they all still had enough time before dinner, to make a run into Jamba Juice. It turned out that Jack and Teddy and Gus had all ridden their bikes to practice.

Before they left, Jack said to Cassie, "I was surprised to see you and Sarah up there."

Cassie told Jack about Sarah's ride over to her house, and the European capitals, and how Sarah had actually surprised her by wanting to come to practice.

"Sounds like she's keeping you off balance," Jack said.

"One big thing I've learned about Asperger's," Cassie said, "is that no matter how many common traits they say there might be, everybody's different."

Jack grinned at her.

"Sounds to me like Sarah's mostly like herself," he said. "You feel like you two are becoming friends?"

Cassie shrugged.

"No clue," she said.

The next day Cassie texted Sarah and asked if she wanted to go to the Cubs' first game. Sarah said no, thanks, and didn't offer an explanation. Maybe she'd just decided there was enough tension and drama on her own team. So Cassie went by herself and watched Jack pitch like a total star against Hollis Hills. He kept his pitch count down, shut them out for six innings, allowing just two hits, one a slow roller toward third that actually stopped before Jerry York could even try to make a play on the ball.

Jack had three hits himself, Gus two. Teddy hit a double. The Cubs finally won 5–0. Mr. Anthony still made too much noise, as if he were somehow afraid that if he went more than a couple of minutes without barking out some kind of instruction, the kids playing the game and everybody watching the game would forget that he was coaching it. But at least there was no drama tonight. Sam, who was starting their next game on Saturday, didn't even play until his dad gave him an at bat in the bottom of the sixth. Mostly Sam saw what everybody else did at Highland Park: what Jack Callahan could do with a baseball in his right hand.

At least, Cassie thought, Sam saw that when he wasn't checking his phone. Maybe it was just another form of his aggressiveness—aggressively checking the phone for messages.

They'd have to wait a few more days to see what it would be like when Sam was the one with the ball in his hand and Teddy was the one catching him. For now, though, the rest of the players on the Cubs had to feel the way Cassie did the other day:

A win was a win.

The way things were going these days, you took what you could get.

EIGHTEEN

As soon as Cassie showed up for her own practice the next day, it was totally obvious that the shunning from Kathleen and the rest of the girls was continuing, in full force. There were times during practice, in fact, when the only noise was the sound of the bat on the ball.

Kathleen and Greta and Allie didn't even talk to one another very much when they were out in the field, as if they were afraid to drop their guards and actually act normal for a change.

When Cassie and Sarah were standing in the on-deck circle together, the way they sometimes did during BP, Cassie quietly said, "You just keep doing your job. I can handle the rest of it."

Sarah turned and looked at her. Her voice wasn't loud, but louder than Cassie's.

"I didn't ask you to handle things for me," she said.

"That's not what I meant."

Cassie's dad had stopped pitching now and walked to the plate to show Lizzie something with her stance, or with her hands. She heard him say, "We need to get you driving the ball again."

"Definitely," Sarah said. "Definitely what you meant. What you meant was that you'd handle things for you and for me both. But I never asked you to do that. Maybe you should just worry about *your* job."

Cassie wanted to ask her where this was coming from, but she didn't. There was enough trouble on their team right now. She didn't need to get into a debate with Sarah Milligan.

Cassie just said, "Trust me. I'm sorry you took it the wrong way."

"I don't trust people," Sarah said.

"I just thought because you wanted me to believe you on that play with you and Kathleen, that you did trust me."

"I don't," Sarah said.

She was staring at the ground.

"I want to stop talking now," Sarah said. "There's always so much talking. Like talking can fix everything. Talking never fixes anything."

Cassie said, "But—"

Far as she got.

"Please stop talking," Sarah said. "Just go hit."

Cassie did. She didn't say another word to Sarah for the rest of practice. She didn't say much to Lizzie and Brooke, or even her dad, for that matter. Nobody else said anything else to her.

When she got home, and even though she knew it was late in Barcelona, she Skyped Angela Morales.

It wasn't that Cassie wasn't getting good support and good advice from the guys. She almost always did. Nobody had better wingmen than she did. But they really were going through their own stuff right now. They were trying to figure things out on their own team. It didn't mean they cared any less for her, or didn't have her back, or wouldn't have been there for her if she'd wanted to talk to any of them or all of them tonight. Jack, in particular, knew her as well as anybody could.

He was still a boy. Cassie grinned as she thought, *Not his fault*. She knew enough about boys to know that they didn't know girls as well as they thought they did. Even though she wasn't exactly an expert on them herself these days.

She needed to talk to Gus Morales's twin sister on this night, because sometimes—no, a lot of times—it felt to Cassie as if Angela were *her* twin too. Angela cared about sports. She was a terrific softball player, which was something that made Cassie miss her even more right now, because there was a part of her that thought that if Angela were around, she would be the one to talk some sense into Kathleen and Greta and Allie and the rest of the ones doing the shunning.

Maybe she would even be helping out with Sarah.

"Buenas tardes!" Angela said when her face appeared on Cassie's laptop screen.

"Oh, great," Cassie said, "here we go from Spanish to English and back."

"It's my heritage," Angela said, grinning, making Cassie feel better already. "Would you deny me my heritage?"

"Yes!"

"Would you be more comfortable with *'Buenos noches'*?" Angela said. "Except that it's after midnight here, which means morning, which means technically I probably should have said, *'Buenos dias.'*"

Cassie didn't say anything.

"What do you think?" Angela said.

"I think," Cassie said, "that if I don't engage, you'll stop eventually."

"Okay, I will, at least for now," Angela said. "So what's up?"

Cassie told her everything that had happened since the last time they'd Skyped. She told her about the way the Red Sox had lost their first game, about the ball in the outfield, which Angela said Gus had already told her about. Cassie told her about Kathleen and the other girls and the team meeting and winning the next game and, finally, about Sarah blowing her off the way she had at practice tonight.

"So she didn't act like a friend."

"Hardly," Cassie said.

"But wait a second," Angela said. "Aren't you the one who's always complaining about having too many friends? And now you're complaining because Sarah won't act like one more? Make up your mind, Bennett."

"I'm not looking to be besties with her," Cassie said. "But I still thought tonight was sort of rude, even if I kind of understood where she was coming from."

"And where might that be, kind of?"

"Well, I do try to control things a little bit."

"You're joking!" Angela said. "How did I miss that?"

Cassie said, "What's the opposite of '*Buenos*' in Spanish, Barcelona Face?"

"That's kind of dark, girl."

"What's dark," Cassie said, "is that now I'm not sure how to even act with her. Do I stop talking to her, the way the other girls have stopped talking to me? And how am I supposed to be a team leader if nobody is talking to anybody!"

"You know you're shouting, right?" Angela said.

"Sorry."

"Don't have to be, not with me," Angela said.

"I know."

She really did feel as close to Angela as she ever had, even though they were still thousands of miles apart. It just made Cassie miss her even more.

"I know you always want to be right," Angela said. "I know how often you think you're right. But you have to realize that what you want for Sarah might not be what she wants. And what you think is best for her might not be best. Or, guess what? Maybe she doesn't know a lot of the same things *you* don't know."

"So I should stop trying?"

"Not what I'm saying. Maybe just stop trying so hard. Just be her teammate, and not her hero."

"I wasn't trying to be her hero."

"You sure?" Angela said.

Cassie wasn't sure. Maybe Angela was right about all of this. Maybe Sarah had been right too.

"No, I'm not sure."

"An unsure Cassie Bennett!" Angela said.

Now she was the one shouting.

"How's that feel?" Angela said.

"I don't know that I want to make a habit of it."

"Listen," Angela said. "I've done a little reading up on Asperger's myself, just to keep up my end of the conversation. Which you could think about doing with your Spanish skills."

"Shut up."

"And the one word that keeps cropping up for me is 'idiosyncratic,'" Angela said. "You know what that means, right?"

"Probably in English and Spanish, both."

"Point is," Angela said, "people with Asperger's are like the rest of us. And you know what that means? *They're all different the way we are!*"

"Jack basically told me the same thing."

"Boy's a genius."

"So what are you telling me?"

"Why don't you let Sarah feel like she's the one in charge once in a while?" Angela said. "She's probably spent her whole life having people try to make her into something they think she should be."

Angela paused, and then said, "Maybe she can take care of herself better than you think she can."

Cassie smiled across the world at her friend. "Thank you," she said.

"You know I love you, right? You know our sisterhood is to the end, right?"

"To the end."

"So I can tell you something else: you're not always the easiest person in the world to get along with either."

Cassie was still smiling.

"*Buenos noches*," she said.

And signed off.

NINETEEN

The Red Sox won their next two games with ease. Cassie pitched one of them, against Rawson. When it was time for her dad to remove her from the game, with the team having just scored three more runs to stretch its lead to 7–2, he let Sarah pitch the seventh inning instead of Allie.

Allie didn't act surprised, or question his decision. Chris Bennett had already told the team he might do some different things with pitching over the next couple of weeks.

"You've probably heard this one before," he'd said. "But you can never have enough pitching."

Cassie had looked around when he'd said it, wondering how many girls on the team appreciated that he was having some fun with one of the oldest baseball clichés in the book. No one seemed to, so Cassie had just said, "I'll bet they came up with that one the same day they came up with a walk being as good as a hit."

Her dad smiled at her. She smiled back. It was as if they were letting each other know that at least they hadn't lost their sense of humor.

For her first time pitching in a real softball game, Sarah did fine. She walked the first batter and gave up a two-out single. But she also had two strikeouts, and induced the Rawson catcher to hit a routine fly ball to Kathleen to end the game. When the ball was safely in Kathleen's glove, Cassie went to the mound to congratulate Sarah. Lizzie and Brooke did the same. The rest of the Red Sox players celebrated with one another.

So nothing had changed. The team was still two teams, trying to play as one. Lizzie and Brooke were still talking to Cassie. They told her that the other girls didn't like it but continued talking to them even as they were ignoring Cassie. It was as if there was some kind of rule book for shunning that they were making up as they went along.

Sarah was back on her own island. She would occasionally talk to Cassie at practice, or at a game. But it was as if none of the time they'd spent together away from the field had ever happened, as if Cassie hadn't made any attempts at gaining her friendship or her trust.

But even though Sarah showed hardly any interest in playing well with others, she was performing beautifully, at bat and in the field. You could count on her making one really good defensive play every game. She had gotten two more hits against Rawson, and two hits in the game before that. And Cassie had noticed that even the shunners paid close attention when Sarah stepped to the plate, as if they had come to expect big things when she did. Cassie was sure none of them would ever admit it, but their eyes were telling them that Sarah had made their team a lot better.

Even though Cassie had been telling herself to give Sarah as much room as she needed, she couldn't help herself after the Rawson game, and jogged to catch up with Sarah and her parents as they walked toward their car.

"Hey," Cassie said as she fell in alongside Sarah, who was about twenty yards ahead of her parents. "Can I ask you something?"

"I know you're going to no matter what I say," Sarah said, and nodded. "People do that a lot. They ask permission, but then they do what they were going to do anyway. They do that a real lot."

"You're right," Cassie said.

"So ask."

"Did I do something wrong?" Cassie said. "Is there something I did that made it like we don't even know each other?"

Sarah stopped. She turned to face Cassie. Cassie did the same. As she did, she could see Mr. and Mrs. Milligan stop too, as if they were giving them both room.

"I don't trust you," Sarah said.

Just like that.

"You don't *trust* me?" Cassie said. "Why not?"

"The other girls are shutting me out," Sarah said. "Why aren't you?"

"First of all," Cassie said, telling herself to stay calm, "I'm not like the other girls. And second, they're shutting me out too!"

She knew she'd raised her voice without meaning to, more out of frustration than anything else. So she lowered it now as she said, "You get that part, right?"

"I'm not talking about that," Sarah said. "I'm not talking about what you want to talk about. I'm talking about what I want to talk about. I'm asking you why you want me if none of them want me. Do you get *that?*"

"I like you."

"I don't believe you."

"But why don't you believe me?"

"Because no one else likes me," she said.

Then she resumed walking toward their car, without another word. Cassie thought: *When she's not running away, she's walking away.*

Or maybe she was just finding every possible way to push Cassie away.

The Cubs almost lost their next game, in Rawson, with Sam Anthony pitching. There was no practice and no game for the Red Sox that night, so Cassie got a ride to the game with Jack's parents, and watched as Sam gave up four runs in the first inning and then two more in the second, before his dad was on his way to the mound.

Jack's dad turned to his mom and said, "That boy looks about as happy playing baseball as I used to look when my parents made me clean my room."

Mrs. Callahan laughed. "You cleaned your room?"

"I'm being serious."

"Well, honey, who looks happy when they're getting hit like this?"

Mr. Callahan said, "It's more than that. He doesn't look like he even wants to be out there. And he certainly doesn't look as if he wants to fight back."

Cassie pointed at the field. "Right now it looks as if all he wants to do is fight with his dad."

Mr. Anthony had put his hand out, asking for the ball, which meant he was taking Sam out of the game. But Sam wouldn't hand it over, even though there were still two guys on, and only one out. Cassie couldn't make out what they were saying to each other, but Sam was doing most of the talking. At one point, the ball still in his right hand, he turned and pointed with it at Teddy, who was standing at the plate, watching them.

Teddy ignored him, simply turned around and started talking to the umpire.

Finally Sam handed the ball to his dad and stomped his way toward the Cubs' bench. As soon as he crossed the third baseline, he threw his glove over the bench, and over the fence behind it.

At this point the home plate umpire took off his mask and was on the move, heading straight for Sam Anthony.

Cassie and Jack's parents were sitting in the bleachers behind the bench. Now they could hear everything.

"Go get your glove, son," the umpire said.

It had landed just short of where Teddy's mom was sitting with Gus's parents.

"I don't need it anymore," Sam said. "I'm out of the game."

"Good thing, too," the umpire said, "or I would have been the one to toss you from the game for doing that."

"It's not like I threw my bat," Sam said.

"Close enough," the umpire said. "Now please go over and pick up your glove."

Behind them Mr. Anthony had been talking to Jerry York, whom he'd brought over from third base to pitch. His back had been to the Cubs' bench as he talked to Jerry. But now he turned and saw what was happening between his son and the home plate umpire. Saw and heard.

He came running from the mound. Cassie thought: *Usually you see managers in baseball running toward the field to jaw with umpires. Now the opposite is about to happen.*

"Don't talk to my players!" Mr. Anthony yelled at the ump.

Cassie looked around. Nobody at Rawson Green was moving, except Mr. Anthony.

The umpire kept his cool. "Excuse me?" he said.

"I run my own team," Mr. Anthony said.

He was right in front of the ump, but his voice was still loud.

"And I'm asked to run this game," the ump said. "And in a game in our league, we don't throw bats, and we don't throw helmets, and we don't throw gloves. Now I want this young man to go collect his glove, so the game can continue."

"He's my son."

"I sort of figured that out on my own."

"What does that mean?"

"You figure that out on *your* own."

Sam still hadn't made a move to go and retrieve his glove. Neither Teddy's mom nor Gus's mom and dad had made a move to pick it up for him. It sat where it had landed.

"How about I go get the glove?" Mr. Anthony said. "Will that make you happy?"

The umpire slowly shook his head. "No, it's your son's glove. He needs to go get it."

It was here that Mr. Anthony, who had somehow moved even closer to the ump, made his mistake. He poked a finger at him, clearly coming into contact with the ump's chest protector.

"You don't tell me what to do," Mr. Anthony said.

"Actually, I can. Now you're out of this game."

"You're throwing me out?" Mr. Anthony said.

"I am," the ump said.

"I don't have an assistant coach here tonight," he said. "You can see that I had one of our kids coaching first base. So who's going to coach the rest of the game?"

An amazing thing happened then.

"I'm the captain of the team," Jack Callahan called out from shortstop. "I will."

And he did.

Then another amazing thing happened, after Jerry York got the first batter he faced to hit a ground ball that Jack scooped up near second base and turned into a double play, and got the Cubs out of the inning.

The Cubs came back.

Teddy got the first big hit, in the top of the fourth, a bases-clearing double with two outs that cut the Rawson lead to 6–3.

By then the Cubs didn't just have a player-coach in Jack, they also had a new third-base coach:

Cassie.

"Need your help," Jack said to her from his side of the bench after both Mr. Anthony and Sam had gotten tossed in the bottom of the second.

"What else is new?" Cassie said.

"Can you coach third?"

"Thought you'd never ask."

When she got down to the bench, Jack said to her, "And, Cass? If you notice anything that could help us, don't hold back."

"Yeah," she said. "That's me, always holding stuff back. Sometimes I keep so much bottled up inside, I'm afraid I might explode."

"You think we can get back into the game?"

"Totally," she said.

"So let's have some fun," he said.

"Finally somebody wants to have fun playing ball!" she said, knowing she was speaking for both of them.

She knew she was taking a risk when she waved Brett home from third on Teddy's double, knowing that you never wanted anybody to make the last out of an inning at home. But she trusted Brett's speed, and trusted her own instincts, and Brett ended up scoring easily when the Rangers' shortstop bobbled the cutoff throw. Teddy took third on the play.

It was here that Jack called for Jerry York to bunt, even with two outs, catching everybody by surprise, starting with the Rangers' third baseman. Jerry deadened the ball perfectly. It died halfway up the line. The third baseman didn't even try to make a throw when he finally barehanded the ball. It was 6–4, which was the way the inning ended.

When Cassie got back to the bench, she said to Jack, "I thought the third-base coach gave the signs."

"You don't know our signs."

"Good point," she said. "But *great* call. A squeeze? Seriously?"

"Thought we could steal an extra run," Jack said.

"*Now* are we having fun?" Cassie said.

"We're still losing."

"Yeah," Cassie said. "But it sure as heck doesn't feel that way."

It didn't. Jerry, who hadn't expected to pitch at all this season, finally tired in the fifth, loading the bases with two outs because of a couple of walks and a rare error by Gus at first base. Jack called time and waved J.B. in from second base to see if J.B. could get them out of the jam, even though J.B. hadn't pitched an inning since last season, when he was still living in Pennsylvania. The score was still 6–4 for the Rangers, but more runs here would probably put away the Cubs for good.

Cassie was sitting on the bench next to Scott Sutter, who'd turned his ankle catching a fly ball the inning before and had taken himself out of the game.

"The only time Jack has ever seen J.B. pitch is in batting practice," Scott said. "And even then, not for very long."

"Your new coach sees stuff other people don't," Cassie said.

Scott grinned. "Even you?"

Cassie said, "I was referring to you guys."

They watched as J.B. threw a fastball and the Rawson center fielder hit a weak pop-out to Jerry at second. The inning was over. The game stayed at 6–4.

"Told you," Cassie said.

The Cubs tied the game in the top of the sixth when Gus hit his first homer of the season, a two-run shot to right. J. B. Scarborough, getting into a groove now, then pitched a scoreless bottom of the sixth. As Cassie ran over to the third-base coach's box for the top of the seventh, she realized she felt ridiculously excited, about a game she wasn't even playing. But this was the way sports were supposed to make you feel.

The bottom of the order was coming up for the Cubs. Max Conte hit a long fly ball to right that looked as if it might get into the gap, but their center fielder chased it down. Gregg Leonard beat out an infield hit to deep short, but then Brett struck out swinging. There were two outs now, the go-ahead run still at first.

J.B., whom Mr. Anthony had moved up to second in the order tonight, walked. Now the Cubs had first and second with Jack Callahan coming to the plate. He was no longer a player-coach in this moment. Just a player.

Jack didn't even look down at Cassie. His focus was on the kid the Rangers' coach had brought in to pitch the seventh. Jack didn't look nervous, or excited. He looked completely relaxed, as if this were exactly where he was supposed to be, and wanted to be.

The pitcher, who'd played first base at the start of the game, threw Jack a ball, away. Jack didn't move as the ball went past him, just gave a quick look to see where the catcher's mitt was when he caught it.

Then came ball two.

If the next pitch was ball three, it meant this was like what the announcers like to call an "unintentional intentional" walk. They were trying to get Jack to swing at a bad pitch, something Cassie knew he hardly ever did, and if he didn't, they were going to put him on and take their chances with Gus, even though Gus had gone deep his last time up against the Rangers' first relief pitcher of the game.

The next pitch wasn't ball three. Maybe the pitcher was thinking Jack would be taking with a 2–0 count. Maybe he thought he could sneak a strike past him. So he threw him a strike, about belt-high, maybe just a little to the outside of the plate.

Jack's happy zone.

He didn't try to pull the ball. He just went with the pitch to right-center, hitting a screaming line drive that was on the ground and skipping past both the center fielder and right fielder before they could cut the ball off, both of them chasing the ball like dogs chasing a car as it rolled all the way to the wall. Gregg scored easily. J.B., running all the way with two outs, scored easily. By the time the ball was back to the infield, Jack was on third with a stand-up triple, and the Cubs, who had been trailing 6–0 when Sam Anthony and his father had left the game and the field, were now ahead 8–6.

Jack should have been out of breath, but wasn't. Sometimes

Cassie got surprised, no matter how hot the day was, when Jack even worked up a sweat. He was smiling as he leaned over to Cassie, gave her a quick low five—so quick that Cassie wondered if anybody else on the field even saw it—and said, "Okay. *Now* we're having fun."

Jack decided to stay with J.B., who pitched a one-two-three bottom of the seventh. The Cubs were 3–1 for the season.

Jack was 1–0 as a coach.

TWENTY

The board of directors for Walton Baseball fired Mr. Anthony as the Cubs' coach the next afternoon.

They said it wasn't because he'd gotten ejected from the game. It was because he had made contact with the umpire. They managed to interview several of the parents who had been at the game, and every one, according to Jack's mom and dad, said the umpire had done nothing to make the situation worse. They thought the umpire had been right, and well *within* his rights, to tell Sam Anthony to retrieve his glove.

It was Mr. Anthony who had made things much worse, according to all the Walton parents at the game. Then he'd put his hand on the ump. The vote, Jack told Cassie, was unanimous.

"What about Sam?" Cassie asked Jack on the phone.

"Far as I know, it's up to him if he wants to stay on the team."

"My dad says they could've given him a one-game suspension for throwing his glove, because you can get that even if you throw your bat accidentally after hitting a ball. Or for throwing a helmet."

"He got off easy," Jack said. "I just think they didn't want it to look as if they were piling on the whole family. Anyway, it's up to Sam now. Or maybe just his dad."

"What do you think he'll do?"

"Honestly?" Jack said. "I think the guy could turn out to be a pretty decent pitcher now that his dad is out of the way."

"Does Teddy want him back?"

"Teddy's a good teammate. In the end he'll do what's best for our team."

Cassie laughed. "Don't you mean after you tell him what's best for the team?"

"Nah," Jack said. "Teddy's too smart not to figure things out for himself."

"Who's gonna coach?"

"Probably one of the other dads."

Cassie said, "They should have you keep doing it."

"Right," Jack said. "Like that's gonna happen."

"I'm serious."

"Unfortunately, I know you are. But Mr. Leonard and the other people on the board will pick the right guy."

Mr. Leonard had coached Jack's team last season, and all the guys loved him. But he was traveling too much to do it again this year.

Jack said, "Actually, my dad and Mr. Leonard are going to coach our practice tomorrow, so we can have a team meeting about the new coach. They say they want us to be part of the process, which is kind of cool."

The Red Sox didn't have practice or a game the next night. Cassie told Jack she was coming.

"One night coaching third," Jack said, "and the girl thinks she can practically take over."

"You should coach," Cassie said. "You know what my dad is always saying, right? That Little League would be a whole lot more fun if we could just get the parents out of the way."

"Can't lie, Cass," Jack said. "You're good."

"*I know,*" she said, with feeling, and ended the call.

• • •

The next night Jack's dad and Mr. Leonard put the Cubs through a practice that lasted about forty-five minutes, just basic stuff, batting practice, infield and outfield, a few situational baserunning drills. But Cassie could see everybody on the field going at every one of the drills hard, smiling a lot, laughing, as if they were all still riding a high from the way the Rawson game had ended.

When they were done, Mr. Callahan and Mr. Leonard asked the players to go sit in the bleachers behind first base.

First Mr. Leonard explained the decision about Mr. Anthony, telling them that no player in the league was allowed to put a hand on another player, and so they certainly weren't going to tolerate an adult doing that.

"What we gathered from talking to some of your parents," Mr. Leonard said, "is that what had been a bad situation around this team from the start simply escalated in Rawson."

"But this is still a good team," Mr. Callahan said. "Potentially a great team. And now we mean to do right by it."

"Some other dads have offered to step in for Mr. Anthony," Gregg's dad said. "Mike Sutter is one. And Bill York. Neither one of them can make a full-time commitment because of their jobs. But they said that if they team up, they can handle it."

"But," Jack's dad said, "we wanted to get some input from you guys."

Nobody said anything at first. The guys on the Cubs looked around at one another.

Finally Teddy stood up.

"I want Jack to coach," he said.

Gus had been sitting next to Teddy. He stood up and raised a hand. "I vote for Jack too."

J. B. Scarborough stood up. "Jack."

Jerry stood up. "Jack," he said.

It went like that, the Cubs standing up one after another, until the only one seated was Jack Callahan, who Cassie didn't think was doing a very good job of hiding his embarrassment, his face even turning a little red, as if he didn't know what to do or how to act.

Cassie stood up now. "I actually had my dad look it up, just for fun," she said. "He said there's no language saying a player can't coach, as long as there's at least one adult on the bench."

The Cubs cheered.

Mr. Leonard said, "But what about you, Jack? This will be a lot of pressure."

Teddy said to Jack, "Uh, Jack, pressure is this thing where you get nervous in big spots."

"Very funny," Jack said.

"Seriously," Mr. Leonard said. "I know you handled things

great for one game. Do you really think you could for the rest of the season?"

"I think I can, Mr. Leonard," he said. "I'll just need a little help."

Just as she had in Rawson, Cassie said, "Thought you'd never ask."

The two dads looked at each other. Mr. Leonard shrugged, and grinned and said, "I'll have to sell it to the rest of the board. But as far as I'm concerned, it's a done deal."

Now the Cubs were cheering and stomping their feet on the bleachers and high-fiving each other. As they did, Cassie looked out at the field.

In the distance, near the playground, she saw Sarah Milligan, hand on her bike, watching them. As the celebration for the Cubs continued, Cassie started walking toward Sarah, and this time she didn't take off.

"Hello," Cassie said.

"Hello," Sarah said, and then asked Cassie why everyone was so happy.

Cassie told her what had just happened.

Sarah frowned.

"Their team isn't like our team," she said. "And our team isn't anything like their team."

"Yet," Cassie said.

"There's a lot about sports I don't understand," Sarah said, and Cassie told her there was a lot she didn't understand too, and not just with sports.

Then Sarah got on her bike and rode off, almost as if she wanted to prove Cassie's point.

TWENTY-ONE

Cassie couldn't go to every Cubs game, or practice. But when she printed out the Red Sox schedule and theirs, she saw only a couple of Cubs games she had to miss between now and the end of the regular season. Fine with her. She was happy to have softball and baseball in her life just about every day for as far as she could see into the rest of the summer. It was a good thing, and not just because both teams kept winning games.

There was something more going on with the girl who had

always prided herself on being so tough, even though she would only admit this to herself:

Spending even more time with the guys was making her feel less lonely.

Because being around her own team did make her feel lonely. A lot. She still loved being on the field, for either practice or a game. Once the games started, she could see that the other players on the Red Sox wanted to win as much as ever. But there was something off about it all. They weren't pulling for one another the way they were supposed to. Even when she and Gus had gotten sideways with each other, even when she'd been worried that the tension between them might pull their team apart, it had *always* pulled together once the game started.

Cassie had finally felt like she was a part of something in basketball, even though she knew that Gus wasn't the only one who hadn't wanted her on the team at first. Right now, though, she didn't feel like a part of anything in softball. And on top of everything else that had happened around their team, Brooke Connors, who'd started taking riding lessons, had managed to fall off a horse, break an ankle, and end her season.

So now Cassie really only had Lizzie to talk to, because even though she'd talked to Sarah that night at Highland Park when Jack had officially become coach of the Cubs, Sarah had once again pulled back, from Cassie and everybody else.

MIKE LUPICA

Through it all, though, the Sox kept winning over the next couple of weeks. So did the Cubs.

And after two games away, Sam Anthony texted Jack and asked if he could return to the team. Jack told him to come ahead. Sam told Jack in the same exchange that he still wanted to pitch. Jack told him he was going to get his chance.

"Do you know what you're doing?" Cassie said.

"Heck, no," Jack said.

"You guys are going good," she said.

"It must have been hard, him asking me to come back," Jack said. "That tells me how much he wants to play."

"But can he pitch?"

"We're gonna find out," Jack said, "aren't we?"

Sam's second game back, Jack started him against Clements, a Thursday night game at Highland Park, and Sam promptly gave up three runs in the top of the first, before finally striking out the last two Clements batters with two guys still on base.

There'd even been a moment, before Sam's last strikeout, when Teddy called time and started out to the mound, before Sam waved him off. Teddy stood there and briefly stared at him, before he turned and went back behind the plate and got into his crouch.

When the inning ended, Teddy was off the field first. When

he got back to the bench and started taking off his chest protector, he whispered to Cassie, "Here we go again."

Sam was getting a drink of water at the fountain behind the screen.

Cassie said, "He didn't pitch that badly. And you gotta admit, the ump wasn't giving him a very big strike zone."

"He still doesn't act like he wants to be here," Teddy said.

"But he *is* here," Cassie said.

What she was really thinking was this: *Maybe Sam is the one on this team who doesn't know how to fit in.*

The Cubs jumped all over the Clements starter, scoring five runs in their half of the first. Jack left Sam in the game. He'd give up another run in the top of the third, but it didn't matter, because everybody on the Cubs was hitting tonight, and by the time the third inning ended, they were winning 9–4. Jack left Sam in there through the fifth. The Cubs ended up winning 12–7. Cassie thought she might have seen Mr. Anthony watching from a distance, behind a tree near the playground. But after Sam was out of the game, he was gone too.

When the game ended, Sam left without saying good-bye to anyone.

The next afternoon Cassie and the guys were sitting on the Walton side of Small Falls, near the bridge that Teddy Madden had been terrified to cross once, before he'd overcome those fears, and a lot of doubts he'd once had about himself. Today they'd all brought sandwiches and were having lunch up here.

"I still don't know why we need that guy," Teddy said.

They all knew he was talking about Sam.

"I think he can pitch," Jack said.

"You must be joking," Gus said.

"Nope," Jack said. "He threw the ball way better last night, especially once he got out of the first."

"Yeah," Teddy said, "this time he only gave up four runs instead of six."

"But he competed," Jack said. "He didn't give up."

"He competed after we scored him a million runs," Teddy said.

"He competed in the first when he struck out the last two guys," Jack said.

Gus said, "You know he's gonna cost us a game, right? And that game might cost us the play-offs."

"He deserves a chance," Jack said. "He could've just quit after the way he acted and his dad acted. I wonder how many teams he's ever played on in his life that his dad *didn't* coach."

"But now you think you can coach him," Gus said.

"I'm lucky I know how to coach you guys," Jack said, smiling.

"J.B. would be a better starter," Teddy said.

"Oh, I get it," Jack said. "Now *you* want to coach."

Teddy turned and looked at Cassie. "Admit we'd be better off without him."

"It is too nice a day and I am having too much fun to spend any more time talking about Sam Anthony," she said.

"He doesn't belong," Teddy said.

"You sound like one of *my* teammates talking about Sarah," Cassie said.

"You're comparing me to them?" Teddy said. "That's cold."

"Tell me how you're different," Cassie said. "You don't just want to freeze out Sam. You want him off the team."

Teddy shook his head. "It's not the same."

Cassie propped herself up on an elbow and smiled at Teddy Madden. It was her way of letting him know that they were always going to be on the same side, even when they were on the different side of an argument.

Cassie said, "If you're the one on the outside, it's always the same."

TWENTY-TWO

The Red Sox were playing the softball team from Clements, called the Astros. Cassie was pitching, trying to continue the Red Sox winning streak and not only get them to 7–1, but tie for first place with the Astros, who came into the game at 7–0.

Cassie knew it was more than just first place being on the line. Amy Lewis was starting for the Astros. And if Cassie was the best pitcher in their league, Amy was 1A. Last season they'd faced each other twice, and Cassie had gotten the wins in both games, first 2–1, then 2–0.

For this one day, everything that had been going on with the Red Sox and was still going on, got shoved aside. It was Cassie's best against Amy's best. Cassie's doing her job was the only thing that mattered, not Kathleen and the Shunners, which was the way Cassie had started thinking of them, as if they were a new girl band. She couldn't worry about them, or her continuing non-relationship with Sarah.

I'm the one on an island today, Cassie thought.

The pitcher's mound.

On the way to Highland Park, her dad said to her, "You're still sure you don't want me to talk to the other girls' parents?"

"No!" Cassie said. Loudly.

She saw her dad grinning. "I'm not sure I caught that."

"Dad, after all this time you really don't know a lot about girls, do you?" Cassie said.

"I'd dispute that," he said, "even though I'm pretty sure you're mother would concur with you."

"If you say something, it will only make things worse."

"And you honestly think that they aren't going to change the way they're acting toward you before the end of the season?"

"Gotta hand it to them, Dad," she said. "They're as stubborn as I am."

Chris Bennett laughed. "Good Lord," he said. "The situation is far worse than I imagined!"

Jack and Teddy and Gus had already taken their seats in the top row of the bleachers behind the Sox bench when Cassie and her dad got to the field. Cassie went up and sat with them. It was one of the times when she wanted to hug them. Not just because they were here. But because they were always there for her.

Teddy said, "Amy Lewis. Your nemesis."

"She's really not my nemesis," Cassie said. "I really like her. And I've always *loved* pitching against her."

"Is the new girl gonna keep catching?" Gus said.

"Maria," Cassie said. "Yeah."

"She's good," Gus said.

"He meant to say 'cute,'" Teddy said.

"First of all, I don't think she's cute," Gus said. "And second of all, even if she did happen to be cute, she's not talking to Cassie."

"I don't blame her," Cassie said. "She's just going along."

Jack said, "When guys were bullying Teddy, the ones that bothered me the most were the ones who just went along."

"I know," Cassie said. "But can we talk about this later? I've got to go deal with my nemesis."

"You said she wasn't."

"I might've lied," Cassie said, smiling at all of them.

She bumped fists with them, one after another. Those were like hugs too. The guys just didn't know it.

Cassie pitched the way she had in the first game of the season, except this time she had a no-hitter going through five innings. If she missed having Brooke behind the plate, she wasn't showing it.

Amy had given up just two hits, one to Cassie and one to Sarah, in the first inning, but none since. The score was still 0–0. The only base runners after the first had come on walks, one by Cassie, one by Amy Lewis.

After Cassie had struck out the side in the top of the fifth, Lizzie walked off the field with her.

"This is the best I've ever seen you pitch in your life," Lizzie said. "And I've watched you do a lot of pitching. Even Kathleen and Greta said so."

"But they wouldn't say it to me."

"That would be against the code," Lizzie said. "They still all agree your stuff is stupid today."

"As stupid as they've been acting?" Cassie said.

Amy blew through the bottom of the Red Sox order in the bottom of the inning. The game stayed scoreless. Cassie managed to get three outs on just five pitches in the top of the sixth, keeping her pitch count down. Then, with two outs in the bottom of the inning, she doubled to left-center, the hardest hit ball of the game by far.

Sarah was up now.

Cassie watched from second as Sarah went through her routine, all her various tugs and taps, always in the exact same order. One time Cassie had walked into the living room as her dad, who loved tennis, was watching Rafael Nadal. He'd made her watch as Nadal seemed to go through his own checklist of tics before every single point.

"Obsessive-compulsive," Cassie's dad had explained. By now Cassie knew that a lot of people with Asperger's were the same way.

When Sarah was ready to hit, she took ball one. Then ball two. From second base Cassie was trying to think along with Amy. Having played against her since they were both nine, Cassie knew how confident Amy was in her own ability, almost to the point of cockiness.

Was she pitching around Sarah, even though Sarah had had just the one base hit back in the first inning? *No,* Cassie thought. Amy had just missed with the first two pitches, and not by very much.

Cassie didn't want Sarah to take a walk. Greta was coming up next. She was a decent hitter. But she wasn't Sarah.

Cassie thought: *If you're gonna be a hitter, be one now.*

Sarah hit the next pitch over the second baseman's head and into right field. Cassie was already at full speed by the time she was halfway to third, and the right fielder knew there was no point in throwing home. Sarah would take second, and the Sox would have another runner in scoring position.

Red Sox 1, Astros 0.

Greta was next. Maybe Amy was still thinking about Sarah's hit, and how it had broken the tie. But the first pitch she threw to Greta was right down the middle, and Greta lined the ball over the shortstop's head and into left-center.

This time, Cassie could see, there was going to be a play at the plate, even with the jump Sarah had gotten.

Cassie had a perfect angle on the play from where she was kneeling in front of the Sox bench. Saw the left fielder reach down, in stride, and cleanly field the ball. Saw the clean transfer of the ball from glove to throwing hand. And saw the ball practically explode out of her hand, on its way toward home plate.

Allie, who'd been in the on-deck circle, was telling Sarah to slide. Sarah did.

But Cassie could see that the throw had her.

She didn't come in with cleats high, the way Sam Anthony had come into Teddy that day at practice. She hit the ground exactly where she should have, and went into a neat hook slide, angling her body into the right-handed batter's box, her left leg going for home plate.

But the Astros catcher had set up perfectly to take the throw on one hop, and put a shin guard down between Sarah's front foot and the plate, and reached down to put the tag on her.

All good, at least from the catcher's point of view.

No, the problem was that as Sarah went sliding through the tag, the catcher's mitt caught her right in the face.

Cassie was already up, off her knees, and running for the plate herself, because she knew that as much as Sarah Milligan hated loud noises, she hated being touched even more.

Before Cassie could get to her, Sarah was already on her feet, coming for the Astros catcher, who was just getting up herself. But Cassie wasn't focused on the catcher. She was focused on Sarah, who had her fists clenched and was in the process of raising her right hand.

"You hit me!" she shouted. *"You hit me in the head!"*

Cassie didn't know if Sarah was going to take a swing at the girl. But she wasn't taking any chances, so at the last second, Cassie launched herself through the air like a football player trying to make a diving tackle on a ballcarrier.

Right play, she thought later, *just the wrong sport.*

Sarah was so startled that somehow she'd ended up

underneath Cassie that she just lay there for a second, before she was shouting at Cassie to get off her.

The umpire totally got what had just happened. She came over, after Cassie and Sarah were untangled, and the umpire was the one helping Sarah up.

"It was an accident, is all," the umpire said.

Sarah's face was red, and her chest was heaving. But she stayed where she was, the umpire's arm around her shoulders as the umpire walked her back toward the Red Sox bench. When she got there, head down, Cassie's dad told her that he was moving Kathleen to center and putting Hallie Sands in left for the bottom of the seventh. Neither one of them had to worry about making any plays out there, because Cassie struck out the side. Red Sox 1, Astros 0. Final.

They'd made it to first place the hard way. When Cassie thought about it, it was as if she'd gotten a save—on Sarah— for her own complete game.

When the game was over, Sarah's parents came over and told Cassie's dad that Sarah had decided to quit the team.

TWENTY-THREE

Sometimes I'm the one who feels like quitting," Cassie said.

"You know you don't mean that," Jack said.

"Don't be so sure."

It was the next afternoon. The Cubs had a game in a few hours. Cassie and Jack and Teddy and Gus were on the dock behind Brooke Connors's house. The Connorses were away, having taken a trip to Cape Cod as a way of getting Brooke out of Walton for a couple of weeks, having seen how hard it was for her to be around the Red Sox now that she couldn't play.

She'd told Cassie that getting a chance to take a step back and see from the sidelines what it was like around their team had made it even harder.

"Everybody seems to have forgotten what it was like at the start of the season and all we wanted to do was talk about making it to Fenway," Brooke said before she left. "But I haven't."

"Remember something, though. If we go, you still go with us."

"It won't be the same."

And Cassie said, "Hardly anything is the same as it used to be."

She reminded Cassie again to go hang out on the dock whenever she and the guys wanted to. Now here they were. There were a few places in Walton where they liked to come and just talk about things. Chop things up, as Teddy said. Other than sitting above Small Falls, this was the place they liked the best, especially on a summer day like this, with the sun high in the sky and no wind to speak of and the water completely calm.

Except, Cassie thought, nothing was calm for long this summer, even when both their teams, Cubs and Red Sox, were winning. And both teams *were* winning.

"Well, one thing I know," Cassie said. "I can't let Sarah quit."

"Not your decision, Cass," Gus said.

"Not saying it is," she said. "But I'm not going down

without a fight." She look over at Teddy. "I wouldn't have if you'd gone ahead and quit your team."

"That wasn't the same," Teddy said.

"Oh, like you not wanting Sam on your team is supposed to be different from Kathleen and the other girls not wanting Sarah?"

"But," Teddy said, "those other girls didn't make Sarah quit. She did that on her own."

"It's not like she didn't have help," Cassie said. "It's like that thing you always hear about in sports, how even one big play at the end isn't the reason you won or lost. A whole lot of stuff had to happen before that. Well, guess what? A whole lot of stuff happened with Sarah—and *to* Sarah—before that play at home plate."

"Gotta say," Gus said, "your play was better."

"*Heck* of a tackle," Teddy said.

"This isn't funny," she said.

"Come on," Teddy said. "I'm just trying to lighten the mood, Miss Dark Cloud."

"I know," she said.

She rolled over onto her back and looked straight into what was pretty much a cloudless sky.

"Explain to me again," she said, almost as if talking to the sky, "how come my team is winning and I feel like we're losing."

Jack said, "Because sometimes it takes more than winning for sports to make us feel the way they're supposed to."

"You guys seem to have figured it all out now that you're coaching," she said to him.

"Figured it out for now," Jack said. "But we've still got our own stuff."

"Like what?"

"Like I need for Sam to start pitching good," he said. "Because if he doesn't, I won't be able to explain to the other guys why I keep starting him and not J.B. or Jerry."

"How do you explain it now?" she said.

"When somebody asks, I just tell them to pay attention to when Sam does pitch good for an inning or two, because he's got really good stuff sometimes."

"Yeah, well the stuff I've got going on around my team is *never* good," Cassie said.

"Gotta admit," Jack said. "You got me there."

"But you'd never quit in a thousand million years," Teddy said.

"No," she said, "I would not. But I still can't let Sarah quit. It wouldn't just be bad for our team. It would be really bad for her."

"How would it be for you?" Jack said.

"It's not about me," Cassie said.

"Really?"

"What is that supposed to mean?" Cassie said.

"It means," he said, "that sometimes I get the feeling that you think that somehow if Sarah fails, you lose."

Jack was sitting cross-legged. Cassie sat up so she was doing the same, and so she could look right at him.

"That makes absolutely no sense."

"Don't get mad," Jack said.

"I'm not mad."

"I meant don't get mad when you hear what I'm about to say."

"I won't."

"You swear?"

"No," she said. "But man up and tell me anyway."

"What I think," Jack said, "is that you're still trying to do right by Sarah and still trying to get her to fit in. But what I don't get is why that's been so important to you from the start. And why somebody you still hardly know is more important to you than a lot of people you do know."

Cassie swiveled her head so she could see Teddy's and Gus's reactions to that. They were both shaking their heads. It meant that for now they were sitting this one out.

Then she turned back to Jack.

"What, you're saying that the other girls are right and I'm

wrong?" she said. "Tell me you're not saying that, Callahan."

"I'm not saying that at all," Jack said. "What I'm saying, and maybe should have said before this, is that you've been acting like Sarah was some game you were trying to win."

Cassie started to answer. Before she could, Jack put out a hand to stop her. "Only, it's not a game with her. And even if things work out the way you want them to, she's still going to have issues. So as much as you like winning, there may not be any winning here in the end."

"Can I say something?" Gus said.

"You don't have to ask permission," she said.

He grinned. "Well, sometimes I do with you."

"Guy makes a good point," Teddy said.

Gus said, "You told us that Angela told *you* that maybe the best thing would be to let Sarah feel like she was the one in charge."

"And I've been doing that!" Cassie said.

In a quiet voice Jack said, "Like when you tackled her?"

"She was about to hit that girl!"

His voice still quiet, Jack said, "Are you sure?"

Cassie took a long time before she answered, and then finally said, "No."

She moved herself back, so that she could face all of them at once.

"You guys think she might have stopped herself?" she asked them.

"Would've been kind of a cool thing for her if she had, right?" Jack said. "Maybe then she would have been the one feeling as if she'd won something."

Cassie hadn't thought about it that way for one second. Hadn't even considered it. In the moment, she'd just made up her mind about what she thought Sarah was going to do and then reacted.

When she had done that, she'd been doing exactly what Angela had accused her of doing:

Trying to be her hero.

"I didn't think," she said.

"Hey," Teddy said. "Happens to the best of us."

"So if you guys are so brilliant, what do I do now?"

"Now, you're probably going to hate what I'm going to say next," Jack said.

"Try me."

"How about you apologize?" he said.

TWENTY-FOUR

Cassie rode her bike over to Sarah's house later, timing it out so she could go from there to the Cubs' game at Highland Park.

It's funny, she thought on the way over. Even though she knew all the different ways to get to Sarah's street, she ended up taking the exact route Sarah had described that day in Cassie's room. She could almost hear Sarah reciting the streets like she was the voice of the GPS woman on a phone.

Cassie thought about calling first. But if she did that, she risked Sarah telling her not to come. And if there was no one home, Cassie had decided she'd ride into town, grab a slice of pizza at Fierro's, and wait until it was time for the Cubs to play the Greenacres Giants.

But when she got to the house, there was the Milligans' car parked in the driveway.

After Cassie rang the bell, Mrs. Milligan opened the front door.

"Hey, Mrs. Milligan," Cassie said. "Sorry to just drop by this way. But I was wondering if Sarah's home."

Kari Milligan smiled. "Soon," she said. "She and her dad are over at the park playing catch."

"Didn't even think to check there."

"She hadn't touched a ball or bat or her glove since the game ended the way it did. But about an hour ago she asked Jim—my husband—if he wanted to go over there. He'd taken the afternoon off from work."

"Well, the way that game ended for Sarah is why I'm here," Cassie said. "I wanted to apologize for what I did. I just assumed . . ."

Mrs. Milligan smiled again. "The worst," she said.

"Kind of."

"Would you like to come in and wait for her?"

"If you don't mind."

"I don't."

Cassie didn't want to put this off. The things she wanted to say to Sarah, she wanted to say today. She didn't think they would keep. The way Cassie had worked it out, if she could get Sarah to change her mind before the Red Sox played another game, then her quitting the team really didn't count.

And maybe the fact that she even wanted to have a game of catch with her dad today was a good sign.

They sat in the living room. Mrs. Milligan asked Cassie if she wanted something to drink. Cassie said she was fine.

"Is there any way I can help you?" Mrs. Milligan said.

"I just don't feel as if I can do anything right with Sarah," Cassie said. "And then even when I feel like I'm doing something right, it goes all stupidly wrong."

"That can happen around here on a daily basis," Mrs. Milligan said. "And I don't just mean once a day."

"Sometimes I don't even know what I'm feeling," Cassie said.

"My guess is sympathy, whether you look at it that way or not, Cassie. Only, that's not what Sarah is looking for. If anything, she's looking for empathy. Do you know the difference?"

"Not really."

"Empathy is when you put yourself in someone else's shoes," Mrs. Milligan said, "particularly if that someone has

Asperger's, and you're trying to get close to them."

"Now I'm totally lost."

"Sarah's the one who gets lost sometimes, trying to identify her own feelings, whether they're about you or softball or the team or something else." Mrs. Milligan clasped her hands in her lap and leaned forward. "The frustration you're feeling is something her dad and I feel all the time. As much as Sarah knows how much her dad and I love her, she still pulls back from us all the time. Often she does it by reflex without even understanding why she's doing it."

"She says she doesn't trust me."

"It's because she doesn't. You have no idea how challenging it was for my husband and me to not only gain her trust when she was a little girl, but keep it."

Cassie said, "I've tried really hard."

"And in her own way, Sarah's tried too. I believe there's a part of her, maybe even a big part, that wants to be your friend. She simply doesn't know how to do it, because she keeps getting in her own way. That's the thing about Sarah that you need to understand: it's not you who can't get through her defenses. It's Sarah herself."

"I've tried every way I can to tell her she doesn't need to be suspicious of me."

"And you could find a hundred more ways. She's still going

to be suspicious. Or maybe 'wary' is a better word. It's like the old joke about not being paranoid, just extremely alert."

"She wanted to know how come I wanted to be her friend when nobody else on the team did."

"And you just have to accept that she's probably never going to be your friend, at least not the kind of friend you're used to. It has nothing to do with her intelligence. Sarah is a highly intelligent person. It's why it frustrates her when she realizes that she's not fitting in. Frustrates her and makes her angry, and even makes her lash out occasionally."

Mrs. Milligan was smiling again, but it didn't seem to be a happy smile. "And then she has no idea how to fix things."

"I thought I could help her fit in, but I was wrong."

"You can't look at it that way, in terms of right and wrong. Black and white. That's the way Sarah looks at things. In her world there is no gray."

"One thing is black and white for me," Cassie said. "She shouldn't quit the team. She's too good to quit."

"She's great, actually," Mrs. Milligan said, looking almost sad as she did.

"Do you think it will help if I apologize?"

"It can't hurt."

They heard Sarah's voice in the front hall then. Her dad was laughing about something, and Sarah was telling him he was crazy. He said he wished he had a dollar for every time some-body had told him that in his life.

Then Sarah laughed.

Cassie wasn't sure she'd ever heard Sarah laugh like that. Or at all.

And in that moment Cassie knew exactly what she wanted to say to her. Maybe what she needed to say.

When Sarah came around the corner and saw Cassie sit-ting there, she stopped. And stopped laughing. "What are you doing here?" she said.

Cassie didn't know why, but she stood up.

"I figured out something," she said to Sarah.

"What?"

"I figured out that it's not you who needs a friend," she said. "It's me."

TWENTY-FIVE

So now you know how I feel," Sarah said.

"Little bit."

"What took you so long?" Sarah said.

She was still standing in the doorway to the living room, arms crossed in front of her.

"Sarah, please be nice," her mom said.

"'Sarah be nice,'" Sarah said. "Sarah be this. Sarah be that."

It was like she was reciting. "If I won't be nice, is she going to tackle me again?"

Cassie just watched. If anybody else, boy or girl, acted the way Sarah was acting right now, even after what Cassie had said about needing a friend, Cassie would have thought she were getting blown off. If Jack or Teddy or Gus tried it, she would have gone right at them and accused them of being rude.

Bottom line?

She wouldn't have let anybody else she knew get away with it. But Sarah wasn't somebody else. She was Sarah. All Cassie could think of in the moment was something she told other people all the time: deal. Meaning deal with it, whatever "it" happened to be. Now Cassie was the one who had to deal.

Mrs. Milligan stood up. Mr. Milligan was behind Sarah. Mrs. Milligan reminded Sarah that Cassie had made the effort to come over to talk and said that now she and Sarah's dad were going to leave them alone to do that.

When they were gone, Sarah said to Cassie, "That's my chair."

"Okay," Cassie said, and moved over to where Mrs. Milligan had been sitting on the couch. They stared at each other for a minute. Sarah still had her arms crossed.

Finally Sarah said, "You shouldn't have tackled me that way. My mom just said for me to be nice. That wasn't nice what you did. That was bad. You made me look bad in front of all the other players. That was bad and wrong."

"I realize that now," Cassie said. "It's why I came over to apologize."

"You keep asking me why I don't trust you? That's why. You don't trust me. Why should I trust you?"

"You're right," Cassie said. "It's why what happened is on me."

"You thought I was going to do something stupid," Sarah said. "People always think I'm going to do something stupid. Don't try to deny it. They do, they do, they do."

"No," Cassie said.

"Yes," Sarah said. She started nodding her head. "Yes, they do. People always say they want me to fit in. But then they don't let me."

It was one of those times when it was almost as if Cassie weren't here and Sarah was talking to herself.

"I did want to do something to that girl. She hit me in the face with her glove. She was the one who did the stupid thing. But I knew better than to hit her. I was just going to tell her she shouldn't have hit me in the face. But that's all. You have to be careful how you touch people, even when you're tagging them out."

Now she looked up at Cassie, as if remembering she was still there. "I don't like being touched."

"I get that."

"Why couldn't you trust me just one time?"

"I should have."

"Now you come here to my house and tell me you want to be my friend," Sarah said. "But how does that work if you don't trust me and I don't trust you?" She gave a quick shake of her head and said, "Who's friends like that?"

Cassie took a deep breath, let it out. "I never thought you were stupid," she said. "But I didn't give you credit for being as smart as you are. Which makes me a little bit stupid."

"You think I didn't know you were pitying me?"

And there it was. All Cassie could think of was what Mrs. Milligan had said about sympathy and empathy. Not only was Sarah smart, but she was smart enough to know pity when she saw it.

"Another thing I was stupid about."

And then Sarah was shouting at her.

"Just let me play my game!"

"Okay," Cassie said, trying to make her voice as quiet as possible, as a way of bringing Sarah's down.

"Let me play my game and you play your game and everybody can play their game."

Cassie smiled. If she was talking about playing her game, it meant she still wanted to play.

"What's so funny?" Sarah said.

Her voice hadn't dropped at all.

"Nothing's funny," Cassie said. "I was just thinking that you don't sound like somebody who wants to quit the team."

"So what if I don't?"

"So don't," Cassie said. "We need you." She smiled again and said, "And I sort of do too. Before long I'll only have my dad to talk to."

"If I do, it doesn't mean we're going to be friends."

"Got it."

"I just want to be a good team player," Sarah said.

"I'm just trying to do the same," Cassie said. "Okay?"

"Okay."

"I can tell my dad you'll be at practice tomorrow?"

"Yes," Sarah said.

Then she told Cassie she was tired of talking now and that it was time for her to go. Cassie did. As she rode to Highland Park on her bike, taking Sarah's route again, street by street, she thought to herself:

Might not have been the win I was looking for.

But it sure as heck wasn't a loss, either.

TWENTY-SIX

Sarah was right.

They weren't friends, at least not the way Cassie had always thought of friends, even though she thought people were too loose throwing the word around. *I'm friends with her,* she'd hear. But did that mean they really were friends, that they could count on each other? That was different, the way her relationship with Sarah was different from any other she'd ever had.

But they were still teammates on what had turned into the best team in their league with two weeks left in the regular season. This year's team wasn't as good as last year's team, Cassie knew that. This wasn't the season she'd expected, or hoped for, wasn't the season she wanted it to be, for herself or for all her teammates. It was the same way with her dad, who admitted even he wasn't having as much fun as he'd had coaching Cassie's teams in the past.

But it was still the season they were playing, and trying to power through. They'd lost their second game of the season, to Greenacres, 1–0, in a game that Sarah had started and pitched really well in. But Kathleen let what should have been a single get past her after Allie had relieved Sarah, and by the time Kathleen ran the ball down, the runner, who'd been on first, had scored the only run of the game. It was a tough way to lose, but they all knew they'd been totally dominated that day by the Greenacres pitcher, a girl named Audrey Gibbons. She gave up two hits, one to Cassie and one to Lizzie, and shut the Red Sox down the rest of the way.

When the game was over, Sarah came over to Cassie and did something she hardly ever did.

She initiated a conversation.

"The girl who pitched for the other team is as good as you," Sarah said, as if stating the most obvious fact in the world.

"Thanks," Cassie said.

"You don't have to thank me. We might have lost today even if you had pitched," Sarah said.

"Might have," Cassie said. "Hope we don't have to face her in the play-offs."

Greenacres was currently third in the league standings.

"Me too," Sarah said. "She's really, really supergood. Maybe even better than you."

"I'll keep that in mind," Cassie said.

"Would it bother you if another pitcher in the league was better?"

"All I can do is play my game," Cassie said.

Sarah seemed to be thinking that over. "Me too," she said.

She went and collected her gear and left with her parents. Cassie felt herself smiling as she watched them walk through the parking lot near the field at Greenacres. Sarah Milligan might not have been the friendliest person Cassie was ever going to play softball with, but Sarah might have been the most honest. You had to give her that.

Their game had started at ten o'clock, and was over by eleven thirty. The Cubs' game at Highland Park wasn't until two, so Cassie had plenty of time to get back there in time to coach third.

She had come to love the job. In her heart she felt as if she were actually doing a lot more than coaching third base. She felt like she was a part of something really cool and really special that was happening with the team. It was something she just felt, the way she thought they all did, that they were a part of some crazy adventure now that Jack had become player-coach. Almost like they were kids who'd taken over the principal's office.

"You guys are the ones who should be playing for a chance to get on television," Cassie said to Jack during batting practice.

The Cubs were playing their second game of the season against Rawson today.

"I don't care about being on TV," Jack said.

Cassie said, "Wait a second. I thought everybody wanted too be on TV!"

"Not me."

"I know," she said.

"This looked like it was going to be one of the worst seasons ever, because of Mr. Anthony," Jack said.

"You hardly ever talk about him."

"But I can with you."

They both knew he could.

"Now it's like everybody can't wait to get to the next practice, or the next game," Jack said.

"Guess what?" Cassie said. "I feel the same way, and I'm not even playing."

Jack grinned. "It's because you finally learned the signs."

"Maybe," she said, "it's because I like being with your team better than I do being with mine."

"No, you don't."

"You don't know that."

"What I know," he said, "is that nothing beats playing. You know when I found that out for real? When I helped coach your team for that little while last season after I quit playing."

Now, that was something two people who felt they could talk about anything with each other hardly ever talked about. It had been such a terrible time for Jack, after his brother, Brad, had died in a dirt-bike accident, and he'd blamed himself for not telling his parents that he knew where Brad, who'd been a risk taker his whole life, was going that night. It wasn't his fault, of course. But if there was one thing Cassie knew about Jack, it was that he was accountable even to a fault.

The whole thing had been so terrible that Cassie felt as if it had happened to her. Because if something hurt Jack, it hurt her, too.

"It would still be cool if you guys got a chance to play on TV," Cassie said.

"Why do I need TV," he said, "when I feel like we're all in a movie?"

He was pitching today against Rawson. He had Sam

Anthony in left field, something he'd done a couple of times before, even though Sam had told Jack he didn't need to be in the lineup when he wasn't pitching, especially now that he'd started to pitch a little better. But Jack told him that he wasn't just part of the team on days he pitched, he was part of their team every day.

And it turned out he was a pretty decent hitter. Cassie and Jack watched now as he put two batting-practice pitches thrown by J.B. over the left-field fence. When he came back to the bench, Jack said, "You know, you've surprised me."

"Why, because I don't stink at pitching now?"

"No," Jack said, "because you don't stink at hitting."

Sam actually laughed. It occurred to Cassie that the sound of Sam Anthony laughing was almost as unusual as Sarah doing the same thing. She couldn't get inside Sarah's head. She'd probably never be able to do that.

But at least Sam Anthony was acting like less of an outsider these days. Her dad always liked to talk about the law of unintended consequences. Maybe one of the consequences for the Cubs now that Jack was coaching was that Sam felt as if he were a part of something too.

More than he ever would have been with his dad coaching the team.

• • •

MIKE LUPICA

The Cubs were in first place alone by now. Rawson was in second, a game behind them. If the Cubs could win today, with only a week left in the regular season, they'd lock up the top seed, and home field for the play-offs. And she knew that Jack wanted that, even if he never talked about it in front of the team.

"Last ups," he told Cassie. "You always want last ups."

"I like our chances today," she said. "The guy who's starting isn't half-bad. He isn't *me*, of course."

"Who is?" Jack said, and then gave her a quick high five and grabbed Teddy for a few more warm-up pitches.

The Cubs scored first when Jack hit his first home run of the season, making it 1–0 in the bottom of the first. The score hadn't changed by the bottom of the fourth, when Cassie turned around and noticed that Sarah was sitting across the field, in the last row of the third-base bleachers. Cassie gave her a wave. Sarah didn't wave back. When Jack took a seat next to Cassie on the bench, she told him about Sarah.

"Looks like the team has added a fan," she said.

"Well, let's see if we can send her home happy with a win," Jack said.

"Good luck with that."

"Getting a win?"

"No," Cassie said. "Making her happy."

Jack struck out the side in the top of the fifth. But in the top of the sixth, he did something he hardly ever did in a close game. He got ahead 0–2 on the Rawson shortstop, elected not to waste a pitch and try to get the kid to chase. He tried to blow a fastball by him, and the shortstop, a lefty hitter, hit one over the right-field fence. Way over.

Just like that, they were tied. When the top of the inning was over, Jack walked slowly back to the bench. But Cassie knew him well enough to know how furious he was with himself, just by the way she could see him taking one deep breath after another. And she knew enough not to say a single word to him. She decided instead that this was a good time to go get a drink of water.

Brett's dad was the adult on their bench tonight. He was the one keeping the pitch count on Jack. When Cassie sat down next to them, Jack was saying, "Where am I, Mr. Hawkins?"

"You're one short of your limit."

Jack turned and said, "J.B., start warming up."

He grabbed his glove and a ball and went behind the bench, and Teddy grabbed his own mitt. Teddy said to Jack, "You okay?"

"Been better."

"I should have made you waste one."

"Nope," Jack said. "On me."

"We'll get a run."

"Better," Jack said.

Not only did they get a run, but Teddy did the honors, a monster home run to the almost identical spot in right field. It was 2–1 going to the seventh. J.B. walked his first two batters, but then he got a strikeout. And then a fly ball to center that was deep enough to advance both runners. Two outs, both Rawson runners in scoring position. The Rawson center fielder, Kenny Wright, was coming to the plate.

As he walked behind Teddy and the home plate umpire, Cassie felt a tap on her shoulder.

Sarah.

Cassie had forgotten she was even at the game.

"I need to tell you something," Sarah said.

"Kind of a bad time," Cassie said. "Can't it wait?"

"No."

"You sure?" Cassie said.

"Is it a bad time if I can help your team win the game?" Sarah said.

"Not sure I understand."

"I like to watch center fielders," she said.

Cassie looked over, saw that Kenny Wright had taken off his batting glove and was putting it back on.

"Okay," Cassie said.

"I watch them really, really, *really* closely," Sarah said, as if she had all day for this particular conversation. "You can learn a lot by not talking and just watching. I know how much you like to talk. I like to watch, especially when they're playing the same position I do."

"Okay," Cassie said again.

Kenny Wright fouled off J.B.'s first pitch to him.

Then took a called strike.

0–2.

"He can't lay off high pitches. Your friend Jack struck him out on really, really, *really* high pitches his first two times up. You should tell the new pitcher to do that."

She walked away, on her way back to the other side of the field.

As she did, Cassie stood up and walked toward home plate, asking for time from the ump as she did.

By now Cassie was used to people watching her in sports. If you were good, and Cassie knew she was good, people watched you. And Cassie knew she liked that, in whatever sport she happened to be playing at the time. Part of the challenge of playing on the boys' basketball team had been knowing that people were watching her more closely than ever.

She wasn't playing now. She was a coach on a team that really wasn't her team at all. But as she walked toward the pitcher's mound, the ump having granted her the time-out, she could feel every set of eyes at Highland Park on her.

Starting with Jack Callahan's.

He met her at the mound, along with Teddy.

"Uh, Cass," Jack said, "kind of got a situation here."

"You told me that if I noticed something to say something, right?" she said.

"And you noticed something?"

"Well, actually Sarah did."

J. B. Scarborough said, "Who the heck is Sarah?"

"Let's wrap this up, boys and girls," the ump called from behind the plate.

"Girl I play with," Cassie said. "Long story."

Teddy pushed back his mask and said, "Really long."

"She watches baseball really closely, and she remembers that this guy at the plate can't lay off really high pitches. Can't help himself. Jack struck him out twice throwing balls nearly over his head."

The ump was slowly walking toward them.

Jack said, "She's right."

"I should have remembered," Teddy said.

"We both should have," Jack said.

"I hate to break this up," the ump said.

Quickly Jack said to J.B., "Throw the next one in the dirt. Teddy will block it. Then throw the next one at eye level."

"I can do that," J.B. said, "sometimes without even trying."

Cassie said, "Well, then, my work here is done."

On her way back to the bench, she gave a quick look at the third-base bleachers. Sarah was in the top row.

Sarah Milligan, she thought, *you better be right.*

J.B., as instructed, threw his third pitch to Kenny Wright in the dirt. Teddy blocked it like a champ.

Now, Cassie thought.

J.B. threw his next pitch on about the same plane as the bill of Kenny Wright's batting helmet. Kenny took a wild, hero swing. Missed it by a foot. Maybe more. Strike three. Ball game.

While the Cubs ran out to celebrate around J. B. Scarborough, Cassie walked over to the third-base side of Highland Park, then made her way up through the bleachers to where Sarah was still seated.

Cassie knew enough not to make a big deal with her about what had just happened. Didn't try to high-five the girl who said she didn't like being touched.

Cassie just said, "You were right."

Sarah didn't change her expression, or show any sign of acknowledging the compliment. It was as if Cassie were now the one pointing out the most obvious fact in the world.

"There's all sorts of ways to show people you're smart," Sarah said. "Like, more ways than most people think out."

"So I am learning," Cassie said.

Sarah nodded.

"You're not the only smart one about baseball," she said to Cassie.

"So I'm learning," Cassie said again.

"You should go hang with your friends now," Sarah said.

Cassie did.

TWENTY-SEVEN

There was one game left for the Red Sox, against Hollis Hills. One game left for the Cubs, against South Haven, new to the league this season.

The Cubs had already clinched the best record. The Red Sox still needed to win. Both games were on Saturday.

On Friday afternoon Cassie and the guys were stretched out around Jack's pool. There was no practice for any of them today, no place they needed to be. A perfect summer afternoon. The only big decision was where to have lunch.

"How come if the girls keep winning, they get to be on television and we don't?" Teddy said.

"Maybe it's because they show so much of the Little League World Series on ESPN," Jack said.

"Or maybe they've finally figured out that girls' softball is more fun to watch," Cassie said.

"I'm serious," Teddy said.

Gus grinned. "She is too."

Jack said, "Hey, if we win the league championship, is it going to feel like any less of a championship even if it's not on TV?"

"Wait a second!" Gus said. "I thought that if something isn't on TV these days, it practically didn't even happen."

"Or on Instagram," Teddy said.

"Or Facebook Live," Jack said.

"I think it started with the Kardashians," Cassie said. "Or maybe all those Real Housewives shows."

"My mom says that if you're being logical, they're actually unreal housewives," Jack said.

"I feel like I've been in one of those shows this season," Cassie said. "*The Real Softball Girls of Walton.*"

"Just without the shouting," Jack said.

"Yeah," Cassie said. "Just a lot of real loud silence."

She was on a lounge chair, just having gotten out of the

water, staring up into the sky, wearing a big pair of glam sunglasses her mom had let her borrow.

She felt a huge sigh come out of her.

"I shouldn't feel this way," Cassie said. "But it kind of bothers me that if we win, a lot of the girls get exactly what they want."

"You mean for *them* to get on TV," Gus said.

"Totally," Cassie said. "They act like complete losers all year, and end up winning."

"But it shouldn't take away from the feeling you'll get if *you* win," Jack said.

Cassie said, "I keep telling myself that."

"How does Sarah feel about this stuff?" Teddy said. "Does she ever talk about the other girls with you?"

"She doesn't talk about much of anything, except softball," Cassie said. "I think she blocks out a lot of stuff, and she's just sort of blocked off the other girls. I think she's so used to being on the outside, she hasn't changed all that much now that she's on the inside."

"You found out what it's like to be on the outside too," Teddy said. "I used to feel that way when everybody used to call me Teddy Bear."

"You know what it's like," Cassie said, "and now I do too."

"Things will get back to normal when we get back to school," Jack said.

"Yeah," Cassie said, "but do I want them to?"

They hardly ever talked about the coming school year, when they'd move over to Walton High and into the ninth grade. Cassie's theory was that they didn't talk about it because they were happy where they were. It wasn't that any of them were afraid of new things, or new challenges. They just liked their world the way it was. They felt secure in that world, even when things weren't close to being perfect in it. She thought of the bridge over Small Falls, the one that had once terrified Teddy, until he finally made it across.

It was like there was a new bridge in front of all of them.

"Things are going to be weird enough in the fall," she said. "I don't need to pack in any extra weirdness."

"So let's change the subject," Teddy said.

"To what?" Cassie said.

"Lunch!" he said.

It was when they were coming out of Fierro's an hour later that they saw Kathleen and Greta and Allie crossing the street, headed straight for them.

"Great," Teddy Madden said under his breath.

"Can we make a run for it?" Gus said.

"I'm not running from them," Cassie said.

"Joking," Gus said.

Cassie thought: *Why not? The whole thing has been like a bad joke from the start.*

But there was no place for them to go. A standoff.

Before they decided on their next move, Teddy said, "Hello, ladies."

He sounded as friendly as if he were running for class president. Or mayor.

The girls turned around. "Are you talking to us?" Kathleen said. She looked at Teddy, then Cassie, then back at Teddy.

"I am!" he said.

It stopped her. It was as if Kathleen and Greta and Allie were so used to not talking when Cassie was around that now they didn't know what to do. Or say. Or didn't know if they wanted to say anything. It was like Teddy had called them out, in the most pleasant way possible.

"Where you guys headed?" Teddy said.

"To get something to eat," Kathleen said.

"Well, as you can see, you're in luck," Teddy said. "Because the best pizza in town is right through the doors behind us."

Cassie gave a quick look at Jack. He was smiling, the same as Teddy.

At least, she thought, *somebody here is having a good time.*

"Well," Greta said, "we're actually not sure what we want to eat."

Cassie couldn't help herself.

"How you guys doing?" she said, knowing how ridiculous that was, since they saw each other almost every other day at practice or a game. But now it was as if they'd been away at camp.

"Fine," Kathleen said.

Greta and Allie nodded. *What a relief,* Cassie thought. *They're all fine.*

Only, nothing was fine, and hadn't been for a while.

"Don't you think this has gone on long enough?" Cassie said.

Just because it had. Because one day of this would have been long enough. Or dumb enough. Or both.

"You started this," Kathleen said.

"How so?"

"By believing her and not me. You're the one who took sides."

"No, Kath," Cassie said. "What started it was a stupid lie about one stupid play."

"I didn't lie," Kathleen said, as dug in here in front of Fierro's as she had been that day.

"You know what?" Cassie said. "I don't even care anymore! It doesn't even matter to me whether you called for that stupid ball or not!"

The words came out hot because she was, and she didn't care whether they were seeing that or not.

"So why are you talking to use now?" Kathleen said.

"You know something?" Cassie said. "I don't have a good answer for that."

"I know why she's talking to you."

It was Jack. He hadn't said a word until now. But Cassie could see that he had their complete attention. She wasn't sure what it was about him that gave him this kind of authority. There was just something about him, and had been for as long as Cassie had been his friend. When Jack spoke, people listened to him.

"She's speaking to you because she's your teammate," Jack continued, "and that's what teammates do."

Kathleen tried to gather herself. Teddy really hadn't called her out. But Jack just had.

"I wasn't speaking to you, Jack," she said, and had to know how defensive she sounded.

"I thought everybody was speaking to everybody, Kath," Jack said.

"This isn't your fight," Greta said.

Jack shrugged and looked around. "Who's fighting?" he said.

"Cassie is," Kathleen said. "With us. And she did start it."

Now Kathleen turned back to Cassie and said, "So now these guys do your talking for you?"

A laugh came out of Cassie. She couldn't stop it. *"These guys?"* she said. "Yeah, Kath, you got me. I needed a posse because you know I never stand up for myself."

"That's not what I'm talking about," Kathleen said. She gave a quick shake of her head. "I don't even *know* what we're talking about."

"Or not talking about," Cassie said.

"But here's what *I* know," Jack said. "You guys have a few more games left to see if you can make it to Fenway, which was supposed to be your big goal. And you might be able to get through the regular season acting the way you've all been acting, but you won't get to Fenway acting that way. So if you're going to come together as a team, now would be a good time."

If Kathleen heard what Jack had said, she didn't show it. But Cassie saw how red her face had gotten all of a sudden. For a moment Cassie thought she might cry.

"You were supposed to be my friend!" Kathleen yelled now at Cassie. "You didn't act like my friend."

And in a quiet voice Cassie said, "You're right. I didn't." She slowly began to nod her head, the way you did if you'd suddenly figured something out. "I didn't know nearly as much about friendship as I thought I did."

"What's that supposed to mean?" Kathleen said.

"Still figuring that out," Cassie said. "Kind of a process."

Then she turned and walked away from Fierro's. She wasn't shunning anybody. She just felt like Sarah Milligan.

She was tired of talking.

Exhausted, actually.

TWENTY-EIGHT

It was amazing, if you really thought about it, considering everything that had gone on.

If they beat Hollis Hills, they really did win the regular season championship. And then they were two wins in the play-offs away from their shot at Fenway.

Yeah. Amazing.

Jack and Teddy and Gus went to a movie on Friday night that Cassie had no interest in seeing, so Cassie and her dad went to Cold Stone for ice cream after dinner. They decided to get it in cups so that they could sit and eat it at Highland Park in the early evening.

When they got to the park, they decided to go sit in swings at the playground, which was empty now. It occurred to Cassie that Highland was hardly ever empty in the summer. But it was tonight. No ball games going on. No kids with their parents. Just the two of them.

"Just like when we came here and ate ice cream when you were a little girl," Chris Bennett said to her.

"Sometimes I wish I still were one," Cassie said.

Her dad laughed. "Me too!" he said.

They sat there in silence for a couple of minutes, until Cassie's dad said, "But here's the thing: as much as I'd like to have those nights back, and have you be little again, I look at the girl you are now, the *person* you are, and I know I would have signed up for that in a heartbeat."

"Thanks, Dad," she said.

They rocked slightly on their swings and ate their ice cream. Cassie noticed the first fireflies around them. She'd always loved fireflies. She wondered sometimes what they did during the day.

"This season has been nuts," she said.

"Well, it hasn't been dull, I gotta admit that," he said. "Your mom told me about how you ran into Kathleen and Greta and Allie today. What was that like?"

She gave him the highlights. Or lowlights.

"Do you think that breaking the ice and at least talking made things a little better?"

"Nah."

"Maybe things will get back to normal when you're all back in school," he said.

"Jack said the same thing."

He pumped a fist in the air. "Then I must be right!"

"I actually don't think that's gonna happen, Dad. Not even sure if I want it to."

"I understand why you might feel that way now," he said. "But unless somebody moves away, you girls are going to be going through high school together. And you might have heard this one, but time *does* heal all wounds."

Her dad leaned over and gently cleaned some ice cream off her chin.

"Teddy says that it should be the other way around: time wounds all heels. He says that's what he wants to happen to the girls who treated me the way they have."

"You know he doesn't really mean that."

Cassie smiled. "Well, maybe just a little bit."

They went back to rocking in silence on their swings.

TEAM PLAYERS

Then Cassie said, "You want to know another crazy thing about our season? I kept telling myself that everything that happened was because of Sarah. But I don't think that anymore."

"How so?"

"I think it's been about me, Dad. I thought Sarah was the one who had to figure out why she was playing and what it really meant to be part of a team. But guess what? It turned out to be me."

"I know it's been a challenge, kiddo. But who loves a challenge more than you do?"

"Nobody," she said. "Even when nobody's talking to me."

"I'm talking to you," he said, reaching over now and mussing her hair.

"I've kind of turned into Sarah."

"I don't think so."

"Oh, I'm not an idiot, Dad."

"Noticed."

"What I mean is, I've had to focus even harder on just playing my game than I ever did before. And it has helped me, watching her, because nobody focuses the way she does."

"She controls what she can control," her dad said. "Except for those times when she lost control."

Cassie took her cup and his, walked over, dropped them into

the trash bin closest to them, and came back.

"You know what the best thing that's happened is?" she said. "I understand better why I play."

"You didn't before?"

"Oh, I always knew that I loved playing and competing and doing well," she said. "But before this season, I'd look at girls on losing teams, ones who didn't have a chance at winning the title or even competing for one, and wonder what kept them going."

"There's all sorts of ways to win in sports," he said. "If I've learned anything, playing and coaching, I've learned that."

"You sound like Jack again."

"Did it ever occur to you that Jack might sound like me?" he said, grinning at her.

She grinned back, and bumped fists with him.

"Kathleen said that I started the fight," Cassie said. "But you know what I've been thinking since I saw her? I'm not fighting with her. I'm just fighting harder than I ever have before, trying to do something great."

"That's my girl," her dad said.

He'd been saying that to her for her whole life. He used to say that when he'd push her on these swings and she'd keep telling him she wanted to go higher. But there was something about the way he'd just said it—*that's my girl*—that made her eyes start to well up.

She stood up. So did he. She put her arms around him and held on tight.

"I've never been prouder of you than I have been this season," he said. "However it comes out."

"Thanks, Dad," she said.

"You're still my little girl. You know that, right?" he said.

"I do," she said. "But we need to keep that between the two of us."

She didn't let go, and neither did he.

TWENTY-NINE

The game with the Hollis Hills Yankees felt like a play-off game, just because it mattered to both teams.

The Red Sox got first place if they won. The Yankees got into the play-offs if they won.

But Cassie wasn't interested in knocking the Yankees out of the play-offs. This wasn't about them. It was about her team. It was about her. She wanted to finish first. Keep fighting.

Cassie was starting today. And her dad had already announced that Allie would start the first game of the play-offs. He didn't say it, but everybody knew that if Allie faltered, Sarah would be the first relief pitcher into the game. By now everybody had seen how much arm she had. Cassie'd even thought that her dad might start her in the play-offs. But when she asked him about that, he said he honestly believed that Sarah was more valuable to them—and more comfortable—in center field. She didn't hate pitching. She actually seemed to like it. But being in center, that had become a part of her routine, the order she liked, as much as anything else.

"And," he explained in the car, "I've coached Allie a long time. And whatever differences you've had with her, that *we've* had with her, she's earned the right to get this start."

"Fine with me," Cassie said. "I'm just worried about my start today."

Her dad said, "Don't worry. Be happy."

"You didn't just say that."

"Kind of."

"Don't be weird, Dad."

He giggled. "Sometimes I crack myself up," he said.

Last season Cassie might have said something to her teammates, as team captain, before a game like this. She would have told them that they needed to finish a job today, finish off the regular season right. She would have told them that if you treat every game like it's important, then the moment will never get too big for you when the games get even more important.

Something like that.

But all of that stayed inside her own head today. From the time they showed up at the field at Hollis Hills, Kathleen and Greta and Allie acted as if yesterday had never happened, and avoided Cassie the way they had been all along. Cassie did what she always did, soft-tossed with Lizzie and Sarah after she'd warmed up for real with Maria, who'd remained the team's regular catcher after Brooke had gotten hurt.

As Cassie and Sarah walked back to the bench, Cassie said, "Good luck today."

"Why do people say that?" Sarah said.

"Good luck?"

"What does luck have to do with anything?" she said. "I don't even think luck is a thing. Do you really think it's a thing? I don't."

By now Cassie shouldn't have been surprised that Sarah Milligan took things as literally as she did. Even something as innocent as a teammate wishing her luck.

"Have a good game, then," Cassie said. "I guess that's what I should have said."

"Then why didn't you?"

Cassie thought: *Maybe my teammates not talking to me isn't always such a terrible thing.*

"Not a clue," Cassie said.

Then she put out her glove, and Sarah touched it lightly with her own, before she went to her usual place at the end of the bench, then walked over to the bat rack to make sure her bat was where it always was.

She didn't believe in luck, obviously.

Just order.

Today there wasn't much luck needed for the Red Sox, because Cassie kept setting down the Yankees in order.

She struck out the side in the first, gave up a hit in the second, struck out the side again in the third. Even the hit she gave up wasn't much of a hit, a slow roller hit to Greta's right. Cassie got over to first in plenty of time, but Greta was a little slow getting the ball out of her glove, and the girl from Hollis Hills beat the play.

It was 2–0 by then for the Sox, because Cassie had doubled in the first and Sarah had doubled her home and then scored on a single by Kathleen. And that's really the way the game should have ended, because Cassie just kept rolling, into the seventh, her pitch count low, determined to finish what she'd started, the game, the regular season. All of it.

In the bottom of the seventh, though, with Cassie still out there, Lizzie kicked a routine ground ball. The next girl bunted, but even though Maria fielded the ball cleanly, she decided to try to get a force at second, and sailed the ball all the way into center field. By the time Sarah ran it down, the Yankees had runners on second and third, with nobody out.

Cassie looked around the bases and thought:

Okay, what the heck just happened here?

But she knew the answer. Sports had just happened. What did her dad like to say? You didn't get to rent today's game. It was her job to figure out a way out of the jam. Lizzie asked for time and started to walk over to the mound. Cassie met her halfway, covered her mouth with her glove, and said, "No worries, Liz. I got this."

"Sorry I got you into this mess," Liz said.

"Shut up," Cassie said.

She went back to the mound and struck out the Yankees second baseman on four pitches. Then got the shortstop to hit a weak pop-up between the mound and first. Cassie waved off Greta and caught it herself.

Two outs.

The Yankee's best hitter, their center fielder, Lexi Garcia, was next. Cassie felt as if she knew her fairly well, having faced her the past two summers. It meant Cassie knew how much power Lexi had and how the harder you pitched her, the better she liked it.

And Cassie knew full well that you had to stay away from Lexi's sweet spot: balls down and in. It was that way with a lot of left-handed hitters. You didn't see it as much with right-handed hitters. But that's the way it was with Lexi. Allie had thrown her that kind of pitch last season, and Lexi had hit the longest home run Cassie saw all year.

It was here that Cassie made the only mistake she'd really made all day. One of the biggest she'd made all season.

She missed her spot completely.

Threw Lexi a pitch that was down and in.

And Lexi crushed it, pulling it to left-center.

Right between Kathleen and Sarah.

Cassie could hear Sarah yelling for the ball all the way from the pitcher's mound, no doubts on that this time. The ball might have been a little closer to Kathleen. But even though both of them had started out running hard for the ball, Sarah had clearly taken charge, as if she were sure the ball was going to end up in her glove, and end this game.

Kathleen then played it exactly the way you were supposed to when you're giving way to the center fielder. She veered to her left, giving Sarah plenty of room, but ready to back her up if somehow Sarah couldn't make the play.

Except.

Except that as she did angle herself to get behind Sarah,

Kathleen's right leg buckled underneath her in a sickening way, Kathleen grabbing for her right knee as soon as she hit the ground.

As she did, Sarah stopped, for a far different reason than she had on the same kind of play in the first game of the season.

She stopped because she was looking at Kathleen and not at the ball, stopped because she was hearing what everybody on the field was hearing: the sound of Kathleen crying out in pain.

As Sarah did, the ball fell underneath her glove, and began rolling all the way to the outfield wall.

Sarah wasn't even watching it. She was already kneeling next to a teammate in trouble, even though it was the teammate who had started all of Sarah's troubles on the Red Sox.

THIRTY

By the time Nell Green came all the way from right field to collect the ball and throw it back toward the infield, Lexi was all the way around the bases with an inside-the-park homer that won the game for the Yankees, and handed Cassie her first loss as a starting pitcher in two full seasons of softball.

Yankees 3, Red Sox 2.

Lexi's teammates, not really focused on what was happening

in the outfield, mobbed her as soon as she crossed the plate with the winning run. As they did, the Red Sox players, and Cassie's dad, and Kathleen's mom and dad, were running toward left-center, where Sarah and Kathleen were.

Cassie beat them all out there.

"Don't move, don't move, don't move," she heard Sarah telling Kathleen. "You'll only make it worse if you do. I hurt my knee one time in basketball and even had to have surgery, and they told me afterward that I only made things worse because I tried to put weight on it. So don't put any weight on it, okay? Don't move, don't move, don't move."

"It hurts so much," Kathleen said, tears streaming down her cheeks.

"Please don't cry," Sarah said. "I hate when people cry."

Cassie's dad, and Kathleen's parents, were there by now.

"Where does it hurt, honey?" Kathleen's dad said.

"Everywhere."

"It'll be okay," he said. "Just don't move."

"I told her that," Sarah said. She looked at Cassie. "You heard me tell her that, right? I told her not to move because it would only make things worse."

"I did," Cassie said. "You did good."

Kathleen's mom was behind her daughter, gently patting her

back. She said they were going to get her to the car and take her to Walton Hospital, which Cassie knew was twenty minutes away, tops.

Cassie's dad and Kathleen's dad asked the girls from both teams, because all the players from both teams were out there by now, to please give them some room. Then the two men helped Kathleen up, as Kathleen kept her right leg completely off the ground. She had stopped crying by now. Her eyes were still red. Cassie's dad asked where their car was, and Kathleen's dad said, "Right behind home plate. Got here late, and had to risk a foul ball busting my windshield."

Cassie's dad always said that only inexperienced softball parents parked that close to the field.

One careful step from Kathleen at a time, the two dads half walked and half carried her toward the infield. As they did, the girls from both teams applauded. Sarah didn't applaud, just stared, wide-eyed, at Kathleen. Cassie thought Sarah might cry too, as much as she said she hated crying.

Then, as Kathleen and the dads got to second base, they stopped. Kathleen turned around, and called out, "Sarah?"

Sarah took a couple of steps forward, as if she'd just been called on in class.

"Yes?" she said.

MIKE LUPICA

lost, of course. She was always disappointed when she lost, and she was now, because she hadn't finished the job. Lizzie could blame herself all she wanted for making an error. Maria, too. Sarah could blame herself for attending to Kathleen while the ball and the game were rolling away from her. But none of them had put that pitch to Lexi in the worst possible place.

No, this was on her.

Kathleen's dad had said he'd call Chris Bennett when he knew something at the hospital. But just the way Kathleen's knee had twisted and collapsed underneath her made Cassie believe that the news had to be bad. She knew enough about sports by now, all sports, to know that non-contact injuries were hardly ever good.

It was a half hour after the game had ended. Cassie had packed up her gear, but she was in no big rush to get out of here, knowing she still had plenty of time to get back for the start of the Cubs' game against the South Haven Mets.

She thought Sarah had left a few minutes ago with her parents. But now Cassie looked up and saw her walking back from the parking lot, past Cassie's dad and the Hollis Hills coach, whom Chris Bennett had once played in high school ball.

"I forgot to tell you something," Sarah said.

"Okay," Cassie said.

"I just wanted to tell you I'm sorry," Sarah said. "I know how much you hate to lose, and I was the reason why we lost today. So I'm sorry for that. I let you down. I hate letting people down, the way you hate to lose. Sometimes I feel like I'm always letting people down, even ones who I know have gone out of their way to be nice to me. And I know you have, even if I don't always show I do or not. I'm not good at showing people what I'm feeling, mostly because sometimes I don't know how I'm feeling."

There was a lot to unpack here, Cassie knew. It was one of her mom's favorite words: "unpack." Sarah was telling her a lot of things at once. Cassie decided to start with the easiest one for her to handle.

"I'm the one who made us lose today, not you," Cassie said. "I'm the one who threw that pitch."

Sarah was staring out to the outfield. "I should have caught the ball."

"You were distracted."

"I lost my focus."

"You had a reason."

"My parents always tell me that my best thing is my focus. It's why nobody ever has to tell me to do that. To focus. It really is my thing. Sometimes I focus so much that I do it too much. But mostly I'm better at focusing than almost anything else.

Other than remembering. You know how good I am at remembering things, right?"

"I remember," Cassie said. "And what I'm going to remember about today is that you did exactly what you should have done: you looked out for a teammate. And by the way? Probably one who's never thought of looking out for you."

Sarah didn't say anything.

"I would have done the same thing," Cassie said.

"It doesn't mean we're alike," Sarah said.

"Maybe not. But maybe more than you think."

Sarah ignored that. Cassie was used to it. Sometimes Sarah responded to what you'd just said, sometimes not. When you had a conversation with her, she was the one making the rules, whether she understood that or not.

Cassie said, "My mom says that just because everybody thinks, it doesn't mean they think alike."

"If you say so."

"And getting back to what you said a few minutes ago? I don't hate losing as much as I love winning."

"That sounds like the same thing."

"It's not."

Cassie looked across the field and saw her dad shaking hands with the Hollis Hills coach. Time to go.

"The only thing I really hate," Cassie said, "is meanness."

"That's another thing we are alike on," Sarah said.

"My dad and I are gonna head back to Walton for the Cubs game. You want to come watch later?"

"Maybe."

She was still staring out at center field. Now she turned and looked at Cassie, with all the focus she'd just been talking about.

"So do you accept my apology or not?"

Cassie smiled. "No," she said.

Sarah said, "I see what you did there."

"Good," Cassie said.

And for one of the first times since she'd known her, Sarah Milligan smiled back at her.

"You're tough," Sarah said.

"Makes two of us."

THIRTY-TWO

It was 4–0 for Greenacres in the semifinals by the time Cassie's dad got Allie out of the game in the top of the fourth. It was Wednesday night. The Cubs would play the next night.

Allie had given up two runs in the first, pitched well for a couple of innings, and then put the first two batters on in the fourth. She got two outs after that, both on pop-ups in the infield, and looked like she might get out of it with the runners still at first and second. But then Marisa Russell, the

Greenacres pitcher, tripled over Nell Green's head in right. A two-run game had just gotten a lot worse. The Sox were four runs behind now, and Marisa was pitching like a total star for the other team.

Suddenly the season was shrinking on them. Even if they somehow managed to hold the Giants from here, they still needed five runs. If they couldn't get them, not only weren't they going to get their shot at playing in Fenway Park, but they weren't even going to make it to the finals.

When Cassie's dad went to take the ball from Allie, he signaled for Sarah to come in from center field. Cassie was on the mound with her dad after Allie left. Allie was on her way out to right. Nell was going to move over and replace Sarah in center.

Chris Bennett said to his daughter, "I was one batter late. I'd convinced myself she was going to get out of it, and then I was going to bring Sarah in to start the fifth."

"I felt the same way, Dad."

When Sarah got to the mound, Cassie's dad said, "You can do this."

Sarah looked at him, acting almost confused by what she'd just heard.

"I know I can," she said. "I have to find out if I *will*."

Even now, things were black and white with her.

Cassie's dad left first. Cassie lingered for just a moment, and said, "Look on the bright side. At least he didn't wish you luck."

Sarah said, "I need to warm up. Please leave now."

"Okay, then."

"Is there any time when you don't want to talk?" Sarah said.

She walked the first batter she faced, the Greenacres right fielder, on four pitches, not one of them being close to the strike zone. So now the Giants had first and third. Still two outs. Cassie thought: *We can't get much further behind, or the only season I'll have left by two o'clock is the one the Cubs are still playing.*

I'll be a full-time coach by then, she thought.

The next hitter for the Giants was their first baseman, Stephanie Rawls. She was the biggest girl on their team and had nearly hit a home run off Allie her first time up.

Sarah finally threw a strike right down the middle. Stephanie took it, as if she weren't going to swing until Sarah did throw a strike. Cassie exhaled so loudly, she was afraid Sarah could hear her at the pitcher's mound.

But then Sarah threw the same pitch again, a fastball down the middle that was a little higher in the strike zone this time, and Stephanie scorched a line drive to Cassie's left. If the ball got past her and into center, the score would be 5–0 and the inning would continue for the Giants. And Sarah Milligan still wouldn't have recorded her first out.

Before it was past her and into center, Cassie dove and got her glove on the ball. She felt the sweet sting of the softball in the pocket of her glove. Where it stayed. As the game stayed 4–0.

Cassie got quickly to her feet, tossed the ball to the infield ump, and jogged off the field, as if what had just happened were no big deal. Even though she knew it was a very big deal.

When she got to the bench, Kathleen was the first to greet her.

By now she'd already had surgery to repair the torn ligament in her knee, and had been sitting next to Cassie's dad at the end of the bench, her cast stretched out in front of her, crutches in the grass next to her. But she didn't use the crutches to get to her feet. She got herself up and put up her hand to Cassie for a high five.

"Don't knock me over," she said.

"Don't worry," Cassie said, and softly slapped her hand.

"That was one of the best plays I've ever seen you make," she said.

"Sometimes there's only one reason you make a play like that," Cassie said. "'Cause you have to."

"Now we have to score some runs," Kathleen said.

"That would be fun," Cassie said.

Just two old friends, Cassie thought, *chopping it up at the big game.* Better late than never.

But nothing changed in the bottom of the fourth, because Marisa Russell breezed through a three-up, three-down inning. Sarah did the same in the top of the fifth. It was still 4–0.

What happened next, though, in the bottom of the inning, happened fast, like a storm blowing across Highland Park, one that started at the top of the Red Sox batting order. Lizzie walked. Allie surprised everybody and laid down a bunt. Cassie doubled both of them home. Sarah doubled home Cassie. Greta singled home Sarah. In a blink, it was 4–4. The Greenacres coach got Marisa out of there. One batter too late.

The game was still tied in the top of the seventh when Sarah walked Marisa, who was playing third base now. Then the girl who'd replaced Marisa as pitcher, Shannon Betts, hit a pop fly to short right-center that Cassie knew Sarah would have caught easily. But Nell and Allie both broke late on the ball, and it dropped between them. Marisa had to wait and see if it was going to be caught, so she only made it to second. It was still first and second, nobody out. If the dropped ball bothered Sarah, she didn't show it, because she proceeded to strike out the next two batters.

Then she walked the Giants second baseman on a 3–2 pitch, even though the pitch looked perfect to Cassie from where she was standing at short.

Just not to the home plate ump.

She called it ball four.

Bases loaded.

And Sarah Milligan was hot.

"That was a strike!" she yelled.

She wasn't looking directly at the ump. She'd actually turned and was facing center field. But the ump had to have heard her, because Cassie was pretty sure everybody at Highland Park had heard her.

Sarah didn't seem to care.

"Totally a strike!" Sarah yelled again.

Cassie asked for time and walked to the mound, even as Sarah continued her loud conversation with herself.

"That was a strike, totally a strike, a strike right down the middle," Sarah said.

At least she'd lowered her voice slightly.

"You can't call that a ball. That is wrong. Totally wrong."

Cassie was at the mound by then, facing home plate. She could see that the umpire, a woman, had taken off her mask. Never good. And the look on her face said that Sarah better not say another word.

MIKE LUPICA

Sarah turned back around.

"Do not look at her," Cassie said, keeping her own voice down.

"You don't get to tell me what to do."

"I'm the captain of the team," Cassie said. "So, yeah, right now I can."

Cassie looked over and saw her dad standing halfway between the Red Sox bench and the first baseline. Cassie gave him a fast shake of her head.

"Are you going to tackle me again?" Sarah said.

"Nope," Cassie said.

"So what do you want?"

"First of all, I want you to shut up," Cassie said. "And second of all, I want you to remember what you told me when I did tackle you, about how I didn't trust you. Well, this time I'm going to trust you to help us win the game. Because you're too good to get thrown out of it."

Sarah was taking deep breaths. Her face was red. But she had shut up, at least for the time being.

The ump started walking slowly toward them, her first sign that this meeting at the mound was about to come to an end.

"You wanted to be a part of this team," Cassie said. "Well, be a part of it now. The last hitter didn't lose us this game. But the next one sure can."

She took the softball out of Sarah's hand, rubbed it up hard, slammed it back into the pocket of Sarah's glove.

"You're the one who needs to stop talking now and pitch," Cassie said.

Cassie didn't wait to see her reaction. She was on her way back to shortstop. Chris Bennett had already taken his seat next to Kathleen on the bench. Sarah threw strike one and then strike two to the Greenacres left fielder, Lily Bates, who then hit a routine ground ball to Cassie's left. Cassie reached down, picked it up in stride, ran, and touched second base herself for the force that ended the inning.

Cassie singled with one out in the bottom of the seventh. The count went to 3–2 on Sarah. Cassie was thinking that maybe the best play for the Greenacres closer was to walk Sarah, then take her chances with Greta, even though Cassie would have moved to scoring position.

She threw Sarah a fastball instead. Sarah hit it over the center-field fence. It was 6–4, Red Sox. They were in the finals. Cassie waited at home plate for Sarah, with the rest of the Red Sox losing their minds behind her.

Cassie looked back at them and said, "Nobody touch her."

Nobody did. They just formed a long receiving line behind Cassie that stretched nearly to first base, all of them chanting Sarah's named.

MIKE LUPICA

As Sarah came down from third base, Cassie grinned and said, "Can I just say one more thing?"

"Go ahead."

"Don't forget to touch home plate," she said.

THIRTY-THREE

Jack had decided that Sam would start their semifinals against the Clements Astros, who'd dropped to fourth place by the end of the regular season. That meant that if the Cubs beat Clements, Jack would start the championship game.

But only if they did beat Clements.

When he told Cassie what he was doing, she said to him,

"Wait a second. Aren't you the guy who says that we're never supposed to look past the next game?"

Jack said, "I think we can beat Clements without me pitching."

"But that means you think we need you more in the championship game, only, we don't know who we're playing in the championship game."

"It's gonna be Hollis Hills," Jack said.

Cassie said, "And you know this . . . how? Rawson did end up with a better record than they did."

"They were always the second-best team in the league next to us," Jack said. "Just took them a while to figure that out. And then there's one other thing?"

"What other thing?"

"I follow some of their guys on Facebook. There's been a lot of chirp about how badly they want us."

"Which makes you want them badly," she said.

Jack didn't say anything. He just smiled at her.

"You're still putting a lot of pressure on Sam," she said. "A couple of weeks ago you said you were thinking about starting J.B. in the play-offs."

"He got too good as a closer," Jack said. "And as for the pressure thing? Pretty sure Sam's been under a lot of pressure since he started in T-ball. I've got a good feeling about this."

Now, after Sam had finished warming up with Teddy down the right-field line before the Clements pitcher, Cassie said to Jack, "You still have that good feeling about your starting pitcher?"

"Ask me in about an hour," he said.

By then they were into the fourth inning, Sam was pitching as well as he had all season, working on a two-hit shutout, and the Cubs were ahead 2–0. Jack had tripled in the first, Gus had doubled him home, Teddy had singled in Gus, Cassie waving him all the way even though there was already one out. She'd noticed during warm-ups that the Astros' right fielder had the weakest arm in their outfield. It was the kind of thing Jack had asked her to notice.

"You didn't even hesitate to send Gus," Jack had said when the inning was over.

Cassie had grinned. "She who hesitates ought to be coaching first," she'd said.

"Is that a thing?"

"Now it is," Cassie had said.

But as well as Sam had been pitching, working quickly, getting the ball back from Teddy and throwing it, he lost it just as quickly in the top of the fifth: walk, walk, hard liner to Jack for the first out, deep fly ball to Gregg Leonard near the fence in right-center that allowed both runners to advance.

Then another walk. Jack made a nice play in the hole to stop what should have been a single to left. But he had no play. The runner scored from third. The bases were still loaded.

And now it was a one-run game.

Jack called time, waved for Teddy to meet him at the mound. But while Sam waited for both of them, rubbing up the baseball almost as if he just wanted something to do, Cassie noticed Sam Anthony staring at something in the distance, where the playground was.

Not *something*, as it turned out.

Someone.

His dad.

Whose right arm was straight up in the air.

It wasn't that Ken Anthony had been prohibited from attending Cubs games after he'd poked the umpire that day and gotten fired as coach. But according to Cassie's dad the league's board of directors had made it clear to him that he wasn't supposed to be involved in the team in any way that could have been perceived as him still coaching them. Even though nobody associated with the Cubs—maybe even including Mr. Anthony's own son—wanted him near the team.

"What he did sent a pretty awful message," Cassie's dad

had said. "So the board sent a pretty powerful message to him. I think he's just stayed clear of the team more out of embarrassment than anything else."

This wasn't the first time Cassie had seen him watching from a distance.

But what was he doing?

In the biggest moment of Sam's season, *was* he trying to coach him?

Sam finally turned away from him when Jack and Teddy got with him at the mound. Jack did all the talking, and was finished before the ump gave them any kind of signal to break it up. Jack ran back to shortstop. Teddy started back toward home plate. But then Sam followed him, tapped him on the shoulder, leaned close to his ear, and said one last thing to him. Teddy nodded. Then Teddy slapped Sam on the back. It had taken a long time, but they'd worked things out the way Cassie and Kathleen and the girls finally had.

Better late than never for them, too, she thought.

Charlie Flores, the Astros' center fielder and their best hitter, dug in at the plate. This was the third game the Cubs had played against the Astros, so by now even Cassie knew how much Charlie loved hitting fastballs. High, low, inside, outside, he didn't care. So in this moment it was Sam's power against Charlie's. Except Cassie was worried, because Sam had clearly lost a little off his fastball. Maybe a lot.

The first pitch was a fastball too far outside for even Charlie to swing at. It was almost as if Teddy had been expecting it out there, because he slid out early to get himself in front of it.

It was fine to waste a pitch. But Cassie couldn't see Sam wasting another and going to 2–0 with the bases loaded. Sam didn't want to walk home the tying run. If he did, Jack would surely call for J.B. Scarborough, even though it was still only the fifth, because the game was on the line right here.

Game, and maybe season.

Sam had been pitching out of the stretch when he'd thrown ball one. But he went into his windup now, and then threw the first slow curveball he'd thrown all day. A big lollipop of a curve that looked as if it took about ten seconds to get to home plate.

Charlie Flores, sure he was going to see another fastball—all Sam had been throwing was fastballs—was completely off balance. But he couldn't lay off a pitch that had to look as fat to him as everybody else at Highland Park.

He was lucky to get even a piece of it, hitting a weak roller to Jack at short. Cassie thought it was trouble when she saw it dying well short of the infield dirt. It should have been a tough play.

Just not for Jack Callahan.

He closed quickly on the ball, barehanded it, and threw

almost in the same motion across to Gus at first. The throw beat Charlie by a step for the third out. The game was still 2–1. Gus Morales hit a home run in the bottom of the fifth to make it 3–1, which was the way it ended after J.B. pitched a perfect sixth and then a perfect seventh. The Cubs were in the championship game.

The first chance Cassie got, she asked Sam what it had meant when his father had had his arm up in the air that way. Sam grinned. She'd found he was actually a good guy once you got to know him.

"You only saw one arm up in the air," Sam said. "I saw two fingers. He was telling me to throw my curve."

"How did you even know to look out there?"

Sam Anthony lifted his shoulders, dropped them, and sighed.

"It was like I could still hear him shouting," Sam said. "Just inside my head."

He grinned again.

"This time I was the only one who could hear him."

THIRTY-FOUR

They played both championship games on Saturday. Only, this time the Cubs played first, against Hollis Hills. Jack had been right. The Yankees had beaten Rawson in their semifinal. The Red Sox game against Greenacres, who had upset Clements and their star pitcher, Amy Lewis, was at three. Because the Sox were the highest seed left, the game was at Highland Park. The Cubs would play at eleven.

So it was a big doubleheader Saturday for Cassie and Jack

and Teddy and Gus. They all knew how special a day like this was, all of them playing with this much on the line. There was no way of knowing when there would be another one like it for them, or if there would ever be a day quite like it.

"There was this great old baseball player, Ernie Banks, who was famous for saying 'Let's play two,'" Jack said, right before he was ready to throw his first pitch. "Guy knew what he was talking about."

"How come you're not acting nervous?" Cassie said. "How come you never act nervous?"

"I do," he said. "I just don't let you see it."

"Same."

"You know when I'm really nervous? Watching you," he said. "It's way worse when you have to watch."

"Same," she said again.

He put out his fist. She reached over with her own and tapped his lightly.

"For now," he said, "let's play one."

After that Cassie watched as Jack tried to take all the nerves out of her, and his teammates, and the size of the game. What she was really watching, she knew, was Jack Callahan just being Jack Callahan. He was going up against the Hollis Hills ace, Logan James, a big lefty who could throw as hard as Jack, if not with the same kind of precision. And Logan was good today.

Jack was just better.

He gave up a single to Logan in the top of the fifth. He'd walked a guy back in the second. Those were the only two base runners for the Yankees. Teddy threw out the guy Jack had walked when the guy tried to steal second. Logan got erased by a double play. So the Yankees still hadn't gotten a runner to second through their fifth inning.

The Cubs finally got to Logan in the bottom of the fifth. Two singles, a double from Jack, a home run from Gus, who was hotter now than he'd been all season. It was 4–0. Cassie never liked getting ahead of herself. But she knew that every single player from Hollis Hills had a better chance of becoming an astronaut before the game was over than they did of getting four runs off Jack.

He was slightly past his pitch count by the top of the seventh. Jerry York's dad was keeping the book today, and keeping track of Jack's pitches, and told him he was sitting on seventy-five, usually his limit.

"I've got a whole year to rest," Jack said.

Mr. York smiled. "You're the coach," he said.

Cassie was with them. "This coach only looks this good because of the guy he's got pitching," she said.

Jerry's dad said, "Go finish in style."

Jack did, striking out the side. When the last out was finally in Teddy's glove, Teddy ran out from behind home plate, tossing away his mask, and nearly knocked Jack to the ground when he jumped into his arms.

"I just always wanted to do that," he told Cassie after the trophy presentation.

By then the parents were all on the field and the Cubs were posing with the trophy. When that was finally over, Cassie said to Jack, "You did it."

"We did it," he said.

"Yeah, well, get back to me the next time a player-coach wins the championship of this league," she said.

"Repeat: we did it," he said. "It's never just one guy. It's never *supposed* to be one guy. At least not when sports work the way they're supposed to."

"You know something?" she said. "You're right."

"*You* want to know something?" he said. "I never get tired of hearing you say that."

"Shut up," she said.

Jack said, "Where you gonna hang out until your game?"

She pointed at him, then over at Gus and Teddy, who were posing for their parents with the trophy.

"Where do you think?" Cassie said.

THIRTY-FIVE

Cassie didn't think of it as trying to pitch her way to Fenway Park. She didn't think about making the sixteen-team tournament and giving the Sox a chance to win the three games that would put them in Fenway.

She just wanted to win this game.

She wanted to win this season.

She wanted to win *that*.

Greta and Allie were talking to her again the way Kathleen

was; the way they all were. They weren't being overly friendly. Things obviously weren't the way they used to be, and might not ever be again. She got that. She even got that no one had apologized to her. Teddy joked that it was clear now that Cassie must have been giving herself the silent treatment.

Cassie didn't even know if today's game mattered as much to the other girls as it did to her. But that didn't matter to her either.

The game did matter to her. As much as any she'd ever played in her life. During basketball season she'd kept telling herself that she wasn't trying to prove some point by playing point guard on the boys' team. But today she knew she was trying to prove something to herself.

Mostly about being strong.

She'd always prided herself on her strength, in sports and everything else. She'd always thought she was strong.

Now she knew.

The last thing to do was win the game.

She had a quiet moment to herself, about five minutes to three. She went down the right-field line and sat in the grass with her back against the wire fence that separated the field from the parking lot. The other players knew enough to leave her alone. So did her dad.

And then Cassie thought about Sarah Milligan. The night before, she'd read up a little more about athletes with autism and Asperger's. She hadn't done it for a couple of weeks. It wasn't as if she thought she would find some big secret that would help Sarah today or help the team, or make things easier. She still wanted to learn. She was still looking for a way to break down the barriers between them, whether it helped in softball or not.

And she'd found this story from *Sports Illustrated* about a basketball player with autism who'd once played for Michigan State. In the story he talked about how much sports mattered to him, and why it mattered.

"You might want to work hard," the player said, "to get better at something you like to do. Sports rewards all that. Trust me, it does."

With everybody, Cassie thought. One more time she'd looked for some truth about Sarah and found one for herself instead. The other thing that jumped out at her from the story was the player talking about the sense of "community" you got from sports.

They'd lost that on the Red Sox, for too much of the season. Now she hoped they'd gotten it back, just in time. She hoped but didn't know for sure.

All she knew was that they were about to find out.

She heard her dad calling to her now, telling her that it was going to be practically impossible to start the game without her.

When she got to him, she said, "Let's do this."

Their season in the league was ending with Hollis Hills, the same as the Cubs' season just had. And the Red Sox season had begun with the Hollis Hills Yankees, a game that had been decided when that ball had fallen in between Kathleen and Sarah. So now they had come full circle. Even the starting pitchers were the same: Cassie and Sydney Ellis.

It was still 0–0 in the bottom of the fifth. With one out, Cassie thought she'd gotten every bit of a Sydney fastball, but their left fielder made a great catch, running toward the line. Then Sarah did catch all of one and hit it into the gap in left-center. Their center fielder tried to make a hero play, diving to her right, but missed. Sarah had pulled a ball over third for a double her first time up, and the left fielder was shading her too close to the line this time up. So she was nowhere near the play. By the time the right fielder came all the way over from the other side of the field to chase the ball down, Sarah Milligan was flying between second and third.

As she got near third, Cassie's dad was windmilling his arms like a crazy person, telling her to try for an inside-the-park home run.

Sarah cut the bag perfectly, not taking a wide turn. She was halfway home when the shortstop's relay throw was on its way to the catcher, Kendall Meany. It was a good throw too. One bounce.

Sarah went into her slide. The ball was just a little bit to the first base side of home when Kendall caught it. Sarah slid neatly away from her, the hook slide that Cassie's dad had taught them all during the first week of practice.

When the tag came, high up on her leg, Sarah was already across the plate.

Safe.

"Out!" the home plate umpire, a man, yelled, jerking his thumb over his shoulder.

Cassie had gotten behind the screen to have the best look at the play. She could clearly see that it was a terrible call. But there was going to be no replay review at Highland Park. There were no television cameras. If the ump said Sarah was out, she was out, even if she was safe.

And Sarah knew she was safe better than anyone else. Maybe Kendall Meany, too. But Sarah *knew*.

Now Cassie watched and held her breath as Sarah got to her feet, still breathing hard after her dash around the bases, her face still flushed.

Hands balled into fists, same as they'd been on the day when she got tagged in the face.

Cassie didn't move. She saw her dad start to walk quickly toward the plate from the third-base coaching box. But Cassie yelled, "Dad!" and put a hand in the air, telling him to stop.

He stopped. Cassie felt as if everything had stopped. Time. Her heart. Minor stuff like that.

The next thing she saw was Sarah turning away from home plate, picking up her bat, and walking in the direction of the Red Sox bench.

She hadn't said a word.

By the time Cassie caught up with her, Sarah had put the bat back into the rack and was collecting her glove.

"You were safe," Cassie said.

"I know that."

No change of expression, no emotion.

"But you didn't say anything," Cassie said.

"I know that, too."

Black and white to the end, in her black-and-white world.

"Why didn't you?"

If Sarah actually smiled, it was there and gone. But when she spoke, she pretty much repeated what Cassie had told her at the mound the game before.

"It's too big a game and I'm too good a player to get thrown out of it," she said.

She ran out to center field. Cassie ran out to pitch the top of the sixth. Game still 0–0. Cassie walked the Yankees' second baseman to start the sixth, then struck out the side after that. She was dealing now. She knew it. They knew it. The Sox threatened in the bottom of the inning, but then Ana Rivera, in right today, fouled out to first with two runners on. It was still 0–0. It felt like the same game they'd played on opening day. Cassie knew her pitch count was starting to get up there. She didn't care. She was going back out there for the seventh, knowing she was going to be an at bat in the bottom of the inning.

Control what you can control. Isn't that what Jack always said?

Well, she was in control of the story now.

She only needed eight pitches to get the Yankees in order. Two ground balls. One strikeout. Time for last ups.

Allie walked to start the seventh against Sydney, who was still in there. The count had gone full on Allie, and it looked to Cassie as if she'd taken a called third strike, because she didn't see a single thing wrong with the 3–2 pitch. But the ump called it a ball. Bad call. One that went their way this time. Sometimes things evened up. Not all the time. Sometimes.

Lizzie put down a perfect sacrifice bunt and moved Allie up to second. Now the winning run was in scoring position.

Cassie was about to leave the on-deck circle when Sarah joined her there.

"Don't worry," Sarah said. "If you don't get her home, I will."

"Thanks for the offer," Cassie said. "But I got this."

Jack was who he was. Cassie was who *she* was. Now she was exactly where she wanted to be. Maybe where she was supposed to be. As she came around behind the catcher and the ump, she gave a quick look up into the stands where Jack and Teddy and Gus were. Teddy and Gus nodded at her.

Jack smiled.

Everything Cassie was thinking, he knew.

Sydney threw her another fastball. This time Cassie got all of it. This time the ball was over the left fielder's head before the girl even had time to turn for it. As Cassie was rounding first, she threw her right fist into the air. Allie could have moon-walked to home plate. By the time Allie did cross the plate with the winning run, Cassie was standing at second base watching the celebration, alone one last time.

When she finally started walking across the infield, Sarah came out to meet her. They met at the pitcher's mound.

Sarah was frowning.

"I don't know how to act," she said. "Sometimes I imagine how things are supposed to look inside my head, almost like there's a picture I'm looking at. But I don't have a picture for this."

"You can try being happy," Cassie said.

"I'm not very good at that."

"It's like a lot of things," Cassie said. "You can learn."

Then they went to join their teammates.

AFTER THE SEASON . . .

THIRTY-SIX

It was the week before school started, which meant the week before ninth grade was starting for Cassie and Jack and Teddy and Gus.

So the last week of summer felt a little different this time. As excited as they were to be making the move to Walton High, they weren't ready for summer to end.

At least not yet.

They were high up on their side of the Walton River, the west side, overlooking Small Falls, noisier than usual before them. There was a good breeze up today, which had the suspension bridge over the water swaying gently in the wind.

"I can't believe that bridge used to make me scared," Teddy said.

"Nobody gets to pick the things that make them scared," Jack said.

Cassie saw just the hint of a smile from him.

"I mean, who knew," he said, "how scared Cassie was going to get pitching at Fenway Park."

"Was not," she said, and leaned over and pinched his arm. Then she smiled herself and said, "Well, maybe a little bit at first."

"Maybe a lot at first," Gus said. "I thought you might have been greener than the Green Monster."

Now Cassie pinched him. Teddy moved away from her.

"Who cares whether it was a little or a lot?" she said. "Did we win the title or not?"

"You did," Teddy said.

"Did we get to play on television, thank you very much?" she said.

"You did," Jack said. "Thank you very much."

The Red Sox had won the two games they'd needed to get to Fenway, one in Hartford, Connecticut, and one in Providence, Rhode Island. Then the games at Fenway were on Saturday and Sunday, before the real Sox returned from a West Coast trip the next day. And the last two games of the tournament had been just like the last two games of their league season. Allie had started in the semis; Sarah had finished. Then in the finals it was Cassie going all the way again, this time against a team from Newton, Massachusetts. She struck out ten batters. The Red Sox won 3–0. Two of the runs had come when Sarah had hit a double off the bottom of the Green Monster.

"Maybe it's the way it had to end," Teddy said. "It was like the two of you against the world one last time."

"She never thought of it that way, trust me," Cassie said.

"How are things now with you guys?" Jack said.

"Pretty much the same," Cassie said. "I forgot to tell you guys that after the championship game was over, she came over and told me she thought I had done a very good job. But that I should remember that the team couldn't have won without her."

"Like you kept saying," Gus said. "Black and white."

"What did you say to her?" Jack said.

"What could I say? I told her she was right. And I told her

that even though she thought I talked way too much—"

"You?" Teddy said.

Now he got pinched.

"That even though she thought I talked way too much, I had to tell her that I'd learned more about how to be a friend and a good teammate than I ever had before in my life."

"You think you guys will stay in touch?" Jack said.

"She's going into ninth along with the rest of us," Cassie said. "You know what? I hope so. Sarah says she tries to picture things the way they're supposed to be inside her head." Cassie nodded. "I can see that," she said. "But it's pretty much up to her."

"Wait, something's not up to you?" Gus said.

"Guess what?" Cassie said. "Even though you guys are always telling me how controlling I am, I learned something else this summer: Sometimes *not* being in control isn't such a terrible thing. Sometimes you just gotta let go and make a leap."

"Like into ninth grade," Jack said.

They were all quiet for a moment.

"It's gonna be the same kids, basically," Gus said.

"Still gonna be different," Teddy said.

"But one thing won't be," Cassie said. "We'll still have each other."

She smiled at all three of them.

Then she pointed across the water.

"Just the next bridge to cross," she said.

"Together," Jack said.

ABOUT THE AUTHOR

Mike Lupica is the author of *The Only Game*, the first book in the Home Team series, and many other bestselling books for young readers, including *QB 1*, *Heat*, *Travel Team*, *Million-Dollar Throw*, and *The Underdogs*. He has carved out a niche as the sporting world's finest storyteller. Mike lives in Connecticut with his wife and their four children. In addition to being a bestselling author, he is a celebrated sports reporter both on radio and in print. You can visit Mike at mikelupicabooks.com.